EDGAR WALLACE

SERGEANT SIR PETER

To Sergeant Sir Peter, Scotland Yard's dangerous and debonair young aristocrat went the Yard's most curious cases from the odd matter of Dr. Lal Singh to the strange matter of the death watch that ticked in an old house . . . to warn of murder.

I0563663

A. L. BURT COMPANY, Publishers
New York   Chicago

PRINTED AT THE *Country Life Press*, GARDEN CITY, N. Y., U. S. A.

CONTENTS

CASE I

THE FOUR MISSING MERCHANTS

CASE I

THE FOUR MISSING MERCHANTS

PETER DUNN walked into his grandfather's study in Berkeley Square, and the old man scowled up at him from over his gold-rimmed pince-nez.

This was in the year '18, when the street lamps were painted black so that wandering German aëroplanes should not be quite sure whether they were over Berkeley Square or Hyde Park, and when Marylebone Road was all lit up like Piccadilly to attract enemy bombs. Happily, Marylebone did not know this.

Peter met the scowl with a large smile.

"No good roasting me, sir. I'm not going to argue with you or say anything unpleasant about the Germans—I've been fighting 'em and they're pretty sporting——"

"Don't let us discuss it," said Sir Leslie, with dangerous calm. "What do you want?"

"Well, sir, I've left the army, and I've no money and no equipment except a knowledge of

3

human weakness. Thank God, sir, I've lived long enough with you——"

"Don't let us quarrel." Sir Leslie's calm was pre-typhonic.

Peter smiled happily.

"Well, the point is this, sir—I've got no profession, and no occupation except getting my leg X-rayed to find odd bits of shrap, and I thought, now that the last of the hardware is out of my system, I might as well do something."

Sir Leslie removed his glasses with offensive deliberation. He was a tall, spare man with a gaunt face and the palest blue eyes.

"And you want me to finance you in a motor-car business—or is it a poultry farm?" His voice was silky—but a sort of hard silk. "Or, possibly, you and a few other optimists are thinking of ranching in Canada? A pleasant occupation: riding expensive horseflesh around a wilderness looking for new faces amongst your calves."

Peter's grin broadened.

"You ought to write a book, sir," he said admiringly. "You've got imagination and a style!"

"Let us confine ourselves to realities," said Sir Leslie, not wholly displeased; "and to simplify matters let me say that I am allowing you five hundred pounds per annum. Beyond that I will not go. You have a certain spurious glamour because you were shot in the leg. A man at my club once referred to you, emotionally, as a hero. I don't think you are a hero. You are what they call in America a nit-wit. Every time I see you I regret that I accepted a baronetcy from this damn government——"

"Let's keep politics out of it," said Peter cheerfully. "I'm going to be a policeman."

Sir Leslie surveyed him dispassionately.

"A what man?" he asked.

"A copper," said Peter. "You know—the blokes who wear helmets and try doors and run in old gentlemen who get chucked out of the Empire."

Sir Leslie winced. It had happened nearly thirty years before. And he was certainly not old then.

"Have you any respect in your system?" he asked.

"None whatever. You're a grouchy devil, and I'm very fond of you. But I don't respect you. You're not harmless enough to be respected. Now, what about it—do I lose that money?"

"If you refer to the five hundred a year—no," said Sir Leslie. "I don't care whether you're a policeman or a postman. I was perfectly sure you'd get a job where the unfortunate taxpayer would have to provide your salary. Good-night, Peter."

"Cheerio!" said Peter, and went out.

Eight years later, almost to the day, Detective Sergeant Peter Dunn came into the office of the assistant commissioner and addressed him familiarly. It had taken various officers of the Metropolitan Police Force all those eight years to accustom themselves to Peter's friendliness. Quite a number decided to remain unaccustomed, and, if his reprimands from outraged superiors had not been weighed down in the balance by the awards and commendations of magistrates and judges, he would have remained plain Constable Dunn. And that not long.

"Sorry to bother you, sir, but I'm in rather a hole. By the way, that Bridlington case is cleared up; we took the son-in-law of the murdered woman this morning, and he made a true and penitent confession. No third degree, I assure you—just a little persuasion of the gentlest kind."

The commissioner pointed to a chair.

"Sit down, Peter—what's the trouble?"

Peter frowned and shook his head. He was

very tall and fair and young-looking, broad of shoulder and long-legged. He was the type that sings in its bath and walks as on springs. As a constable he had taken to the station, unassisted, Wilfred Lamb, a notorious beater of policemen, wives, and miscellaneous citizens. And the divisional surgeon worked through the night like a sempstress, putting stitches into Wilfred where and as they were required.

"My grandfather's dead—good old boy. Got tight on vintage port and fell down the stairs. A glorious death. I believe he has left me a quarter of a million—*and* the baronetcy. I could keep very quiet about the quarter of a million, but the baronetcy is a label—I can't duck it. 'Sergeant Sir Peter' is too silly, so I'll have to clear out. And after all the amazing knowledge I've accumulated—it's a dead waste."

The commissioner nodded.

"Your chief charm is your immodesty," he said. "Yet for once I'm in sympathy with you. You *are* a brilliant policeman, and I don't know how we'll find somebody to take your place. I'll see the chief and try to wangle something."

A week later Detective Sergeant Sir Peter Dunn was passed to the Reserve. And from time to time he was called to New Scotland Yard to assist in certain investigations, receiving for his services fees which about paid the licence on his twenty horse-power Rolls and left a little over for cigarettes.

Peter knew Dr. Lal Singh. He had prosecuted him once for obtaining money by a trick, and had failed to secure a conviction. The doctor was a little round-faced Indian with a London degree and no practice. He was a clever surgeon, one of the cleverest that had passed through St. Giles's Hospital, but there was a prejudice against his colour, and men of his own race avoided him because he had a sharp tongue and an invincible weakness for being paid in advance for his services. He lived in lodgings near Gower Street, and had his surgery in a slum off the Edgware Road.

Undoubtedly he could have made, by certain illicit practices, quite a large income, but he was superior to the importunities of dope peddlers and others. Possibly he took up clairvoyance to save himself from starvation. This he practised first at his lodgings, hiring a sitting room for his séances, and afterwards in a Bayswater flat. For money began to come to him in respectable quantities, and he was able to rent and furnish an apartment near Westbourne Grove.

Hither came many ladies of society and ladies who were not in society, and members of the younger set who had been told how perfectly marvellous this seer was. And Dr. Lal gazed into crystals and saw tall, fair men who loved his clients, and short, dark women who were working to rob them of their husbands. And he told the discontented young matrons that they would be married twice and have two children, a boy and a girl, and would be shortly going on a long journey which would bring them great profit.

One day a tall, fair man called on Dr. Lal and was told that he would inherit a title and a vast sum of money.

"How the devil did you know that?" asked the astonished Peter.

"Recognition of distinguished police official and private knowledge of circumstances," explained Dr. Lal, showing his white teeth in a smile.

It was his jest to ape the style of his less educated compatriots. He dropped into good English now.

"I do not charge for my services, Sergeant," he

said, and waved his podgy hand to a side table
near the door. On this was a large box of Benares
brass, and above it a small printed notice:

"*No charge is made by Dr. Lal Singh for his
demonstrations. Money placed in this box will be
distributed to such charities or employed for such
purposes as he may determine.*"

2

The prosecution which followed was none of
Peter's business. He had been detailed for a duty
which he carried out gladly, for he was the Yard's
authority on human weakness and was a tower
of strength to the *modus operandi* (or, as they
call it, "M. O.") department.

He rather liked the little doctor, and was glad
when the prosecution collapsed. After the case he
went down to Bayswater and had a talk with
Dr. Lal.

"I don't want to go back to India. I have
hundreds of odious relations, and to tell you the
truth I am not *persona grata* with the ruling
political organization in India. I should be
'boycott' and humbugged. Here there is opportunity for brainy man even if handicapped by
excessive colour."

"What will you do now?" asked Peter.

There came a strange gleam to the brown eyes of the doctor, and he tapped his nose with a coppery finger.

"I have a truly brain-turning idea! It requires capitalistic help, but what a success is promised if project is satisfactorily pursued! My skill, my studies, the poetry of my imagination——"

"Are you going to be a bookmaker?" asked the interested Peter, but the little doctor did not reveal his dream.

"Money can be made with celerity," he said earnestly. "I shall appeal to certain human emotions—the most prevalent ambition in the bosom of mankind! I can do this thing better than any man, and for obvious reasons. As a boy I enjoyed the dubious advantage of association with certain magical fakirs of India. Some of their deeds were so much nonsense and chicanery. On the other hand, there was wheat amidst the chaff of their so-called knowledge. I set you a puzzle, mister! Disintegrate the same!"

The clairvoyant business languished after this, but although the frugal doctor sold up his furniture and let his flat, Peter suspected that poverty had nothing to do with the flit. Soon after Dr. Lal closed his surgery in Edgware Road, and the next thing Peter heard about him was that he had drawn a prize in the Calcutta Sweepstakes —some six or seven thousand pounds. Peter wondered if he would exploit his brain-turning idea now that he had capitalistic help.

All this was ancient history when there came to Scotland Yard three inquiries concerning the lost City men.

Peter came up from Southampton in response to an urgent wire and interviewed the chief constable.

"I want you to take this case, Peter," said the chief. "You will be nominally under Crowther, but you'll have a free hand. Here are the facts."

The first fact was Thomas Henry Middlethall, of Middlethall, Merton & Payne, silk merchants, of the City of London.

Mr. Middlethall was a rich bachelor, who lived in Fitzjohn's Avenue, Hampstead. He was a man of fifty-six, with artistic tastes, and was well known in theatrical circles. He had financed one or two musical shows, was to be seen in the more sedate of night clubs, and on these occasions generally accompanied a pretty young actress. It was not always the same lady.

He had left his house one day, saying he would be away not more than ten days. A month, two months had passed, and he had not returned. A letter had been received by his partners, written in his own hand, saying that he intended taking a longer holiday, and asking if he might be spared. Four weeks after his disappearance there was a curious happening in Fitzjohn's Avenue.

It was a Wednesday night, and of the four servants he employed three were absent from the house. On Wednesdays he invariably gave three servants an afternoon and an evening off.

The servant in charge of the house was a middle-aged housemaid, a woman named Keating. She was not in the servants' hall, where she should have been, but in a little room opening from the first landing at the head of the stairs. It was, in fact, Mr. Middlethall's private snuggery, and there were certain forbidden books on his bookshelf which it was the ambition of his servants to read. These were behind a locked grille fastened to the front of the bookcase, but Peter gathered on investigation that the grille could be opened very easily, and every servant in turn had profited by his absence to sample the volumes printed "for private circulation only" whenever opportunity offered.

3

Engrossed as she was, she heard the sound of a key turning in the outer door, but thought it was the cook returning and did not stop reading. Presently she heard another sound—another key was being turned. This time it could only be in the lock of Mr. Middlethall's study.

Very alarmed, she put down her book and, opening the door, listened. She heard nothing, and, gaining courage, she went out onto the landing. There was a dim light burning in the hall. Mr. Middlethall was conservative enough to use gas as an illuminant.

As she looked over the banisters she saw a man emerge from the study. At first she thought it was Mr. Middlethall. That gentleman affected a peculiar method of dressing which bordered upon the eccentric. She recognized the rather long jacket and the shepherd's plaid trousers— but the wearer was not Mr. Middlethall. He was a much younger man, and thinner.

Too horrified to scream, she stood motionless and watched the intruder pass into the street. From where she stood she could see through the fanlight a car waiting outside. He had hardly disappeared from view when the car moved off.

Miss Keating seems to have shown a presence of mind rare in such circumstances. She called up the police station, and in a few minutes was telling her story to the divisional inspector. The study had been left unlocked, one of the desk drawers had been opened, and on the floor the inspector found a long envelope, the red wax seal of which was broken. It had obviously contained a new cheque book, posted from Mr. Middlethall's bank. The police instantly communicated with the bank, traced the cheque numbers, and gave instructions that no cheque taken from this book should be honoured.

This took a little time, as did the interviewing of general managers, and before the stop order went forth the first of the cheques had been cashed at a City branch of the bank. Apparently Mr. Middlethall had an arrangement whereby his cheques could be cashed at any of four branches. The cheque was in his handwriting and it was indubitably his signature. Peter made a microscopic examination, and the result left no doubt in his mind that this was not a forgery.

The next day brought a letter from Mr. Middlethall, obviously written in some haste, with no evidence that it had in any way been dictated. It was addressed to the manager of the bank, and ordered that functionary to cash any cheque not exceeding five hundred pounds at intervals not shorter than a fortnight that might be drawn on his account. It bore a London postmark—S. E. 1.

"That's genuine, too," said Peter, interviewing his immediate superior.

"He may have been kidnapped and kept a prisoner somewhere," suggested Crowther.

Peter shook his head.

"You can't mistake it for anything but what it is—a note written spontaneously. Look at the spelling mistakes and the overlining."

"Has he drawn any cheques since he's been away?" asked the puzzled inspector.

This was one of the first inquiries Peter had made.

"None," he said. "That's one of the curious features of the case."

It was on that day that the story of the second disappearance came to headquarters. This time it was a Mr. George Grives, an eminent solicitor in the City of London, a clubman, and something of a *bon vivant*. In many respects his history ran on parallel lines with that of Mr. Middlethall. He also was something of a ladies' man, and had once figured in a case which nearly resulted in his being struck off the rolls. He had a flat in the West End, where he entertained extensively. He was something of a dandy.

He had left his office, telling his managing clerk that he was going to Aix for a ten days' cure. On the tenth day the clerk received a telegram, handed in at London, telling him that Mr. Grives had returned but was leaving that night again for Aix.

Nothing was thought of the matter until the managing clerk mentioned the fact casually to a City detective who had called to make inquiries concerning a case of fraudulent conversion. The officer reported to his chief; the news was telephoned to Scotland Yard; and within an hour Peter was in the office. He learned nothing, except that Mr. Grives had a very close friend, one Charles William Sedeman, a wholesale provision merchant, with a warehouse and office in Tooley Street.

"He'll probably know more about Mr. Grives than any man in London. I really don't think there's anything wrong, Mr. Dunn." (Peter was always known as "Mister" in the course of his inquiries.) "Very probably the governor has——"

It is not necessary to repeat the libellous suggestion of Mr. Grives's managing clerk. He spoke from knowledge, and had a wide experience of his middle-aged employer's flightiness. It struck Peter as a very possible solution, as he was driving to Tooley Street.

Mr. Sedeman was not in his office, and was unlikely to return that day.

"May I see his secretary?" asked Peter.

It was a long time before admission was gained to this important official, a pallid young man with large horn-rimmed spectacles, who spoke rather preciously.

"Mr. Sedeman? I am afraid you won't be able to see him, Mr.—ah—Dunn. Mr. Sedeman is taking a holiday. The work here has been very heavy in the past six months. You probably know what happened to the bacon market in March."

Peter not only did not know, but was not aware that bacon had a market. He was interested to learn that bacon had been doing things which had sprinkled the heads of many provision merchants with large silver threads.

"I didn't know bacon did that sort of thing—not good bacon," said Peter. "Where is Mr. Sedeman staying—has he gone to Aix?"

The secretary hesitated.

"Well," he said rather reluctantly, "originally Mr. Sedeman went away for ten days——"

"Eh?" Peter stared at him. "Ten days? Was that his original intention? When did he leave?"

The secretary gave him a date. It was five days after the departure of the lawyer.

"And what happened?" asked the detective.

"He decided to extend his holiday for another month."

"Did he telegraph you to that effect?"

The young man was obviously uncomfortable.

Well no, to be exact he didn't. He sent a letter by a messenger, who asked me if I would send Mr. Sedeman's cheque book. By the way, he was supposed to be staying at Bognor, but I have reason to believe he never went there. That, however, is a matter which is not quite my business, and it is outside my duties to make inquiries as to Mr. Sedeman's destination. The messenger brought a letter, and in face of the order I could do no more than give him, in a sealed envelope, Mr. Sedeman's private cheque book. What made it so queer was his colour."

"The messenger's colour?" asked Peter quickly. "Was he dark?"

"He was very dark," said the young gentleman in a hushed voice; "in fact, he was an Indian."

It was only at that moment that Peter connected Dr. Lal Singh with this mysterious transaction. He described the little doctor faithfully, took the secretary with him to Scotland Yard, and there produced, from his own private collection, a photograph of the clairvoyant surgeon. He was instantly identified, and a call was circulated through London and the provinces, asking for information concerning the whereabouts of this sometime seer.

4

The secretary was able to furnish Peter with a photograph of the vanished Sedeman, and later that day this was supplemented by photographs of the other missing men. Peter examined them critically in the presence of his chief.

"They're not exactly oil paintings, are they? Wicked old devils, I should imagine."

"Why did they all decide to go away for ten days and extend their stay?" frowned Crowther. "That to me is the oddest part of the business. Are they all bachelors?"

"Only Middlethall. The other two are Benedicks."

"Happily married?" asked Crowther.

Peter smiled cynically.

"Yes—they're living apart. I very badly want to meet Lal Singh," he said, after a moment's thought. "I have an idea he's going to tell me something that will give me a laugh."

Inspector Crowther smiled grimly.

"If you find these birds in the river with their throats cut, you won't be so amused."

"I'm not so sure," said Peter. "It doesn't take much to make me laugh."

The following day the Manchester police sent through an inquiry. Mr. Pinchin, a wealthy cotton broker, had been missing from his home for two months. His home was the best hotel in Manchester, where he maintained permanently a suite of rooms. It was not unusual for him to go away for months at a time; in fact, he had often gone to America with little or no warning to his office. So that when he did not return at the appointed time the office was not particularly worried. It was the slackest period of the year, most of the office staff were on holiday, and the police were not notified until the bank questioned a cheque for four hundred pounds which had been presented and paid. In this case the broker had left no address, giving no clue to his destination. The only certain thing was that he had left for London, after which all trace of him was lost.

He did not go to the hotel where he usually stayed when he was in town, nor was he seen by his London agent. Like the other three, he had vanished into the earth.

Peter went up to Manchester by the first available train and saw Mr. Pinchin's accountant, who apparently was in the know as regards all the broker's secrets. The visit to Manchester was not wholly unproductive. Peter learned that the day before he disappeared Mr. Pinchin had very carefully cut out an advertisement from a London newspaper. He had been interrupted in the act and had shown some confusion, and had ordered the interrupter, who was an office boy, out of the room.

Again the detective managed to secure a photograph of the missing man.

"It is," said Peter, describing the photo to his chief over the phone, "the face of one who has warmed both hands before the fires of life and got slightly scorched. Will you get me a copy of *The Megaphone* for the eighteenth of July, and have it waiting for me when I arrive?"

He reached London, to learn that news had been received of Dr. Lal Singh. A manufacturing chemist had received from him an order for a very deadly and little known Indian drug, and this had been supplied and forwarded to what the police afterwards discovered was an accommodation address. The drug had been collected by the doctor personally. It was not the first time such an order had been received by the chemist. In his books Peter traced no fewer than five deliveries in as many months.

The copy of the newspaper he required did not arrive until late that night, and Peter sat up till two in the morning, reading advertisements one by one, and trying to find in them a certain sinister significance.

He made his discovery in the early hours of the morning, and wrote a carefully worded letter on a sheet of notepaper bearing his own private address. And all the time he wrote he laughed, once so violently that he blotted the sheet before him and had to make a new start.

An answer to his letter came the following evening (Peter had used the name of his butler), and early one hot summer morning Peter Dunn took train for Barnham Junction, which is in Sussex.

He expected to find the little doctor on the platform, but instead he found a very attractive and capable young woman.

"Are you Mr. Herberts?" she asked. "The doctor has sent the car for you."

There was a little two-seater outside the station; the girl seated herself at the wheel and invited him beside her. Half an hour's drive through the most delightful scenery brought them to a rather imposing villa which was hidden from the road by high box hedges, carefully trimmed. They passed through the gate and up the drive, and there under the portico, waiting to receive them, was the most urbane of Indian doctors, wearing a spotless white jacket, and rubbing his hands in anticipation of new revenue.

He saw Peter, and his jaw dropped; but he recovered himself instantly.

"If you will accompany me to my holy of holies," he said, not without dignity, "explanations can be offered."

"No explanation is necessary. I want to see three or four gentlemen who I presume are living in this house, and whose absence is causing their friends a little anxiety," said Peter.

The doctor hesitated; then, walking quickly ahead, he turned the corner of the house onto a broad lawn.

Four men were playing bridge in a rustic

summerhouse, and though Peter had seen the photographs of all, he could recognize none.

"Here's the advertisement." Peter pushed it across the table to Chief Inspector Crowther, and the big man fixed his glasses and read:

"FOR MEN ONLY.—*Why be plain through life? In ten days I can change most unconvincing countenances to the most youthful visage. Consult me secretly.*"

The address of an advertising agency followed.

"That is all there is to it," said Peter. "These fellows went in for a beauty treatment—a sort of bloodless face lifting. I've no doubt Lal Singh added to his surgical knowledge a few things he'd learnt in India. The trouble with Lal Singh was that he was a jolly sight too successful! I've seen these fellows, and the change is amazing —so amazing that they dared not go straight back to their circles of friends, for fear they were not recognized. Dr. Lal has been complaining bitterly of their ingratitude. With his astringent lotions—I discovered the property of the Indian drug he bought—and his treatment, he cut all signs of age from their faces so effectively that they demanded to be put back where they were. It must be a horrible discovery to find you're looking like somebody else. Poor Grives is going abroad for two or three years; he says he dare not show himself in the Courts till the effect of Lal Singh has worn off."

"What I can't understand," said Crowther, "is why Middlethall was prepared to pay more than the others——"

"Take a good look at Middlethall's photograph," said Peter.

CASE II

THE DESK BREAKER

CASE II

THERE is a regular and steady flow of foreign dossiers into Scotland Yard. They are written in a variety of languages and deal with ladies and gentlemen who have done things which they should not have done. Peter Dunn made a practice of studying those documents which came from the United States, for he was compiling for headquarters a general review of the *modus operandi* followed by criminals operating outside the British Isles.

In due course he came upon a short and unflattering biography of Lew Stillman, written by an unimaginative officer of Police Headquarters, New York City, who, if he lacked literary style, had a passion for facts. Peter studied the photograph which accompanied the document, and memorized the face. He duly noted that Lew was a British citizen, which made him a little more difficult to trace than if he had been of alien origin, and compelled a record of his presence and movements at the nearest police station.

There was no need to trace him, for Lew was not "wanted" by the police. His dossier was forwarded as a precautionary measure, because the New York police rather imagined that some day or other his life story would be interesting to their comrades who lived on the Thames.

To Lew's documents they attached others which dealt as frankly with the past misdoings of Al Stephini and Hoofer Genelli and "Tag" Murphy, and several other low-down men, who lived dangerously but well on the proceeds of their illicit professions.

By a curious coincidence Peter met one of these gentlemen mentioned so unfavourably the very week he made the acquaintance of the Garden City of Collingwood. In real life things happen that way.

Peter had left Scotland Yard about four o'clock in the afternoon and was walking along Piccadilly to his house in Berkeley Square. That a detective sergeant should live in Berkeley Square was of itself a fantastic improbability; that he should be a baronet of the United Kingdom was too absurd to think about. But if grandfathers leave titles and fortunes, and grandsons desire to remain detective sergeants, such anomalies must exist.

He had reached the corner of Berkeley Street when he saw a man standing on the edge of the pavement waiting for the traffic to pass. He was a tall, olive-faced man, with a large Roman nose and a prominent chin. There was a large and glittering diamond on his little finger—Peter saw this as he lit a cigar.

"'Lo, Hoofer. Staying long?"

Hoofer Genelli looked round slowly and surveyed the detective lazily.

"You have the advantage of me," he said.

"You bet I have, Mr. Genelli," said Peter. "I'm Detective Sergeant Dunn, C. I. D."

"Is that so?"

Mr. Genelli was not apparently perturbed; he had spent the greater part of his life appearing unperturbed in embarrassing moments.

"Well, I'm glad to meet you, Mr. Dunn. Yes, my name's Genelli—just arrived from America . . . stopped off on my way to Paris. Don't remember meeting you anywheres, Mr. Dunn."

Peter did not attempt to explain that his

recognition had anything to do with a very detailed description which included:

"Big nose and chin; scar left cheek; wears diamonds."

"Take a little walk with me," said Peter.

Mr. Genelli hesitated and fell in by his side. At the nearest police station Peter discovered that Hoofer's papers were quite in order, and they had a little heart-to-heart talk.

"You'll be leaving for Paris very soon, I expect, Mr. Genelli? London is very quiet—you'll find Paris a much brighter city."

"Who told you I was here, anyway?" demanded Hoofer. (He had once been a professional dancer, hence his soubriquet.)

Peter ignored the question. If gentlemen of Hoofer's antecedents did not know that there was an interchange of confidences between the London and New York police departments, they were singularly unimaginative.

It was on the Saturday of that week that Peter struck Collingwood and its amenities.

2

Collingwood was not a garden city by pre-destined plan. It was officially a suburb of

London, and had begun as a sprawling village of picturesque, if insanitary, cottages which clustered about a church and the Bunch of Grapes inn. It developed in the late 'eighties by the creation of a number of interesting little estates varying between eight and three acres, and in the odd corners of these holdings grew a few avenues of artificially designed homes.

There was nothing vulgar about Collingwood; it had neither slum nor problem. Its sidewalks were broad and cemented, its lime avenues were chaste and pretty. Most of its shops and stores were in Old Collingwood, through which the North Road runs, Collingwood proper, the aristocratic Collingwood, lying at the end of a long avenue, remote from the noise and the petrol fumes and fatalities of that great highway.

Peter became acquainted with Collingwood through one of those little accidents which throw people literally and figuratively together. He was coming back from York, driving a very high-powered, super-charged German car, and it naturally irritated him to be held up in one of those narrow stretches on the North Road—which was afterwards widened—by a car of microscopic dimensions which maintained itself, despite his honking and the harsh, imperative summons of his horn, on the crown of the road and would budge neither left nor right. Then, at last, he detected a movement to the side, which he took to be an invitation, and shot his car through the gap; the driver of the small car, at the same moment, decided to return to the crown of the road. There was a terrifying crash, the splintering of glass, and the small vehicle was lifted bodily and deposited on a grassy bank.

Peter put on all his brakes and, stopping with a hideous jar, jumped from the car and ran back to give first aid. The little road bug was beyond that. It lay over drunkenly, minus one wheel and its offside running board. But the occupant was unhurt, save for a scratched face, which bled alarmingly.

He was a tall, thin, not especially pleasant young man. Obviously he had had the benefit of a university education and the breeding of a gentleman, for all his offensive comments were uttered in cold blood with a certain pedantry which was very annoying.

"My dear chap," said Peter testily, "if you hadn't pulled out as I was passing——"

The young man would have cheerfully bled to death rather than forgo the opportunity of explaining the strength of his legal position, but

Peter cut him short. He introduced himself as a police officer, gave first aid, which was reluctantly accepted, and, having secured the assistance of a passing scout to take the remnants of the car to the nearest garage, he forcibly pushed his victim into his own machine, bullied his address from him, and came to a neat little house in Collingwood.

It stood in a quarter of an acre of ground. There was a small square of tidy lawn in front, and, outwardly at any rate, it was one of those prosperous little homes that are to be found by the hundreds of thousands throughout the length and breadth of England.

He rang the bell, and almost immediately the door was opened by a girl who wore a large blue wrapper. She was by far the loveliest young woman Peter had seen for many a day, even in that unbecoming costume.

She stared from the bandaged man to Peter, and her face went pale.

"It's nothing serious," said Peter.

"Nothing serious!" The icy venom in the young man's voice was almost startling. "You'll learn whether this is serious or not. I've never seen a more brutal disregard of the rights of the road——"

She took his arm and led him into the house. Peter was following, but the man turned.

"I don't want you in here—you keep out. Take his name and address, Lydia: I'm too ill to bother with it."

He jerked his arm impatiently from the woman, and Peter heard his feet sound hollowly on uncarpeted stairs as he made his way to the back of the house.

She stood in the half-opened doorway, a picture of discomfort.

"I'm awfully sorry. Is my husband's car very badly smashed?"

She did not ask him whose fault it was that the accident had occurred, and in some way Peter divined that she knew who was in the wrong. It struck him as remarkable at that moment that she did not ask him into the house. She had something to hide; she stood on the doorstep, the door so closed that he could not see inside the passage.

"I'm afraid it is badly damaged, but you are covered by insurance?"

She shook her head.

"My husband never insures. He—he is rather peculiar about things like that. Will you give me your name and address, please?"

He took out a notebook, wrote it down, and tore out a leaf. He was handing it to her when a querulous voice came from the house.

"What's the delay? Are you adding another trophy to your collection? You don't imagine I'm going to wait here all the afternoon? I want some tea."

She almost snatched the page from his hand, and before he knew what had happened the door was closed upon him.

He walked back to his car, interested but not greatly puzzled. His experience as a police officer had taught him that it was impossible to take the lid off any house without discovering ugly little elements of discord.

3

As he got into the driver's seat he was aware that there was an audience to the scene. A man was standing by an oaken gate on the other side of the road. As he turned the car and came opposite, the man signalled him and he came across to the sidewalk. He was a short, florid man with a wisp of yellow moustache.

"Has that bird been smashed up?" he asked. "That was always coming to him!"

Peter stared at his interrogator and brought

the machine to a standstill; but apparently the man did not observe his surprise.

"Too proud at thirty—that's what's the matter with him. They had the sheriff in their house last week—took every stick of furniture. They couldn't take the car because it doesn't belong to him. That girl's worth forty thousand of Mr. Walter L. Glynne. All that he does is run round with a necktie showing he went to a swell school. He's the biggest sucker I've met in years—falls for anybody who can tell him a tale. Say, if that guy was rich you wouldn't be able to get into this street for con. men. Is he hurt?"

"Not badly," said Peter.

"I'm sorry," said the little man. He looked towards the house that hid his unpopular neighbour and smacked his thick lips. "She's a peach, eh? One nice little girl."

"Met a friend of yours recently," said Peter, interrupting the rhapsody. "Hoofer Genelli."

The man stared at him.

"You don't say!" he said slowly. "Is old Hoofer in town?" And then quickly: "Hoofer who? I don't know any Hoofers, mister."

"I'm merely telling you that I met him in town," said Peter. "How long have you been living here, Stillman?"

The man was looking at him through narrowed lids.

"Nearly a year, I guess," he drawled. "So you're a detective, eh? You've got nothing on me. I'm a British citizen, born in T'ronto."

Peter changed the subject.

"What does Glynne do for a living?"

"Nothing," said the other, obviously relieved that the conversation was switched to a more pleasant topic. "He just goes around in a mechanical push-cart; borrowed it from a friend who didn't know any better."

He thought a moment; then:

"Come inside, mister?"

Peter got down and went into the house with him. It was small, but comfortably furnished.

"Will you have a drink? . . . Tea, then?" He rang the bell. "It's a wonder you fellows have got any nerves left. I'm getting the habit myself."

A neat maid in black brought in a tea tray.

"Ever seen work like that?" Stillman handled the delicate lace tea cloth. "I'll bet you haven't. Handworked. I've got three of them. And mats——"

Peter Dunn was not to be led completely off the subject by Mr. Stillman's enthusiasm for

fine needlework, and for ten minutes he questioned, admonished, and advised.

"Say, don't you worry about me." Lew's smile
was bland and confident.

"I'm not worrying so much that it will keep
me awake at night," said Peter.

Before he left they got back to the subject of
Mr. Walter Glynne, and Peter had one piece of
information which explained the cryptic remark
which had been barked at the girl from the head
of the stairs.

"Jealous? I should say he was! I wouldn't
have that man's disposition for a million dollars.
She never goes out of the house except when he's
with her. He thinks she's running after every
man she meets. That's the kind of boy he is.
If he only knew——"

He stopped and chuckled, and then, seeing
Peter's cold eye upon him, hastily disclaimed
all that was sinister in his innuendo.

"That's no light baby, don't worry! Straight
as a line. But what I say is, Mr. Dunn, what's
the use of sticking close to a grouch like that,
when you could have all the money in the world
you want, eh? Do you know how they live?
They've got two little beds they bought from a
junk dealer, a couple of chairs, and a table.

She washes the curtains herself—sits up all night from sheer pride so that none of the neighbours see the curtains are down. The house is hers; he'd have sold that, only the trustees wouldn't allow it."

Peter carried away from Collingwood an unhappy memory of the poor little girl in the blue wrapper. He had a vague idea of sending her money anonymously, but realized, if all Lew Stillman had said was true, that it would bring her little benefit.

He made a few inquiries and learned that Stillman had not exaggerated when he had described the husband as a wastrel. He did not drink, had no apparent vices, except a colossal vanity which was expressed in a profound contempt for the commercial classes. He had written poetry, and had sought a short way to wealth, having as his guide an outside broker, who had stripped him of his own meagre fortune and as much of his wife's property as was realizable.

It was surprising how many people knew of Walter Lister Glynne, though it did not amaze Peter, who had discovered before that most people's lives are an open book for those who trouble to turn the pages.

There came to him a letter from Mr. Glynne's

solicitors and the threat of an action at law—
this was one of the young man's most expensive
hobbies—and he had turned the matter over to
his lawyer when Collingwood again obtruded
into his daily life.

There were three little communities, of which
Collingwood was the centre: Helstone was
one, Digbury Park was another, and Cornford
Heights was the third; Cornford village, being
situate at least fifty feet higher than any of its
neighbours, was entitled to the "Heights."
Digbury Park and Collingwood lay just inside
the Metropolitan Police area, and as such came
within Scotland Yard's sphere of influence. The
superintendent sent for Peter one morning.

"Do you know Collingwood?" he asked.

"Do I know it!" said Peter scornfully.
"There's a lawyer there who writes me twice a
week, and I think I mentioned that our friend
Lew Stillman is in residence in that area."

"You know his record—is he a burglar?"
asked the superintendent.

Peter shook his head.

"No, he's everything but," he said.

The superintendent took up a little pad of
papers and handed them to his subordinate.

"You might go down and make a few inquiries," he said. "In the past six months there has been a series of peculiar burglaries committed in this neighbourhood, and the Hertfordshire police have asked us to investigate. It's evident that the same gentleman is operating in every case."

Peter turned over the sheets.

"What have they taken?"

"Nothing," was the unexpected reply. "That's the odd thing. In every case they have left silver and valuables which they couldn't very well have missed, and in every case the writing desk was broken open and papers searched. Usually the fellow who's been doing the job has waited until the householder has been away, and the suggestion is that he knows their habits and is more or less acquainted with their plans. In no case has money been stolen—that I want to impress upon you."

Peter took the documents to his office and read very carefully the police reports. In every affair entrance had been made through a side door and only two rooms in the house had been searched—the study and the bedroom. Once a pocketbook had been taken, but no other property.

He began his investigations that afternoon,

called at a house in Digbury Park and interviewed the occupant, a well-to-do bachelor
stockbroker who lived with his sister. He was
evidently a man of comfortable means. The
house was large and the grounds fairly extensive.
He could give no information that threw any
light on the mysterious visitor.

"My sister was away at the seaside when it
happened, and I was staying in town at my club.
The house was empty—my sister had the maid
with her, and the cook was on her holiday. The
queer thing is that they didn't steal a very
valuable silver statuette which stands on my
writing table; and, what is stranger still, they
left the money which they found in one of the
drawers they forced."

The burglary had happened three months
before, and the broker was rather surprised that
the police were resuming their investigations,
and should consider the case important enough
to send a man from the Yard.

Peter looked over the house. He saw nothing
till he came to the dining room.

"What is this?"

He pointed to an oblong strip of lace that lay
on the polished surface of the table. For a second
the stockbroker looked a little uncomfortable.

"That? Well, that's just a sort of—I don't know what you call them," he said awkwardly.

Peter picked up the edge of the flimsy thing and saw here a beautifully worked coat of arms. He had seen the same design on the tea cloth in Lew Stillman's parlour.

His next call was on a middle-aged widower who had a tiny house on the edge of Collingwood, and here again no explanation was forthcoming for the burglary, which had almost been forgotten by the owner.

"No, nothing was taken—except my bank pass book. The poor devil must have thought he'd got hold of a prize. As a matter of fact, the pass book was returned to my bank three or four days later. As you know, when the bank sends out a book it usually encloses a printed envelope for its return. This was used and posted in London."

Again Peter made an inspection of the house, and again made an interesting discovery.

4

It was eight o'clock that night when he came back to Collingwood and knocked at the door of Gleneagles, by which magnificent name Mr. Lew Stillman's modest villa had been christened by its builder. He knocked and rang, but no answer came. A servant of the next house, who was gossiping in the dusk with a young man, volunteered a few facts.

"We don't often see him. He usually comes in by the back way. There's a little lane at the back of the house," she said.

"Are his servants out?"

Here she was a mine of information. They did not sleep in the house, Mr. Stillman preferring complete privacy between sunset and dawn.

Peter went back to the house and rang again; there was no answer. He went round to the back of the house and found the back gate locked.

It was grossly improper of him, since his affairs were in the hands of lawyers, to call upon one with whom he was engaged in litigation. Nevertheless, he crossed to the pathetic little house which held the mean secrets of the Glynnes.

He pressed the bell, but apparently it was out of order, and the sound of his knock echoed hollowly. He heard the movement of light footsteps in the hall, and the door was opened a few inches.

The house was in darkness, though from somewhere above came a tiny glimmer of light.

"Who is that?"

It was Lydia Glynne's voice. Then apparently she recognized him.

"Is it Mr. Dunn?—My husband is not in. Please don't stay!"

There was a note of agitation in her voice.

"When will he be back?"

"I don't know. You won't think I am very rude if I turn you away, will you? Only my husband doesn't like me to receive visitors."

She was on the point of closing the door when he stopped her.

"What's the trouble, Mrs. Glynne? Perhaps I can help you."

He heard a quick sigh.

"No, I'm afraid you can't—I'd rather you didn't wait."

She was almost incoherent in her anxiety for his departure, and he could do no more than bid her a good-night which was cut in half by the closing of the door.

He intended seeing Glynne that night, whatever happened, but it was vital that he should see him in the presence of his wife.

Rain was falling when he turned into the narrow lane that ran along the back of the houses opposite. As he did so he thought he saw a figure disappearing into the darkness ahead of

him. It might have been an occupant of one of
the other houses; apparently the lane was frequently used. He walked along to the end and
found himself on the main road of Collingwood.
There were a few cars in sight; the red tail-light
of one was disappearing in the direction of
London as he looked.

For a quarter of an hour he waited, but there
was no sign of Glynne, and, turning, he walked
back along the dark lane. He was twenty yards
from the entrance of Stillman's house when he
heard the scrambling of feet against wood; a
dark figure appeared over the top of the fence,
dropped into the lane and ran. He came from
Stillman's house, and Peter sprinted in pursuit.
The man ran fast and he could not gain on him.
Darting up a very narrow passage between the
two houses, he flew across the road and for a
second was lost in the darkness. The door of
Mr. Glynne's house slammed as he reached the
outer gate. He knocked, but no answer came.
He knocked again more loudly.

"Who is there?" It was the girl's voice, husky
with fear.

"Open the door, Mrs. Glynne. It is Sergeant
Dunn."

"I can't open the door."

"Open the door. I saw your husband come in and I want him."

The conversation could be carried on in a low voice, for the door was glass-panelled. He heard the key snap, and, pushing past her, closed the door behind him.

"Have you a light?" he asked the shadowy figure.

"No." Her voice was quivering. "The electric light is cut off—my husband isn't well. I'm afraid he's fainted. . . ."

And then Peter heard her sob.

"Oh—I'm glad you've come—that somebody's come!"

He took an electric torch from his pocket and flashed it along the bare boards.

"Where is he?"

She led the way, pushed open a door that led to the back room, and he went in.

Walter Lister Glynne lay, an inert heap, on the ground. Stooping, Peter turned him over and gasped. There was blood on the man's hands and on his face where the hands had touched. The sleeves of his coat were redly wet. He heard a scream behind him.

"O God! What has he done?"

"Bring a lamp—you've got one upstairs. Or wait here—I'll get it."

He ran upstairs and brought down a small paraffin lamp and put it on the table of the unfurnished dining room. Glynne had recovered; he was sitting, his face buried in his hands, shivering and whimpering. Peter shook him by the shoulder.

"Who was it—Stillman?"

"Dead," shivered Glynne hysterically. "Terrible . . . ! He was sitting at his desk. I touched him, and when I put the light on it was horrible . . . ! I didn't do it. . . . I swear I didn't do it! I went to find the letters she's been writing to these men. I know she's been writing to them and visiting them. You—you!" he screamed, pointing to the white-faced girl. "I've been looking for them——"

"We know all about what you've been looking for," snarled Peter. "You've been looking for the love-letters that your wife never wrote, you poor worm!"

He turned to the girl.

"Wash him—he needs it," he said, and flew out of the house.

He found a policeman, and together they went

to the back of the house opposite and mounted the fence. When he switched on the light in Lew Stillman's room he saw something which was not nice to look upon. Stillman had been shot through the head at close quarters. His hand was still gripping the gun he had drawn but had had no time to use.

5

They arrested Hoofer at Waterloo Station that night, when he was on the point of catching the boat train for Southampton, and he accepted his fate philosophically.

"Lew got his," he said. "He sent three of our gang to the chair when he turned State's Evidence, the rat! Then he bolted for England. We've been waiting for him—my brother was one who went to the death house. If I hadn't caught him in London one of our boys would have picked him up in Paris."

A day or so later Peter had an interview with his chief.

"The curious thing was, I was expecting Glynne to burgle Stillman's house that night. The man was insanely jealous, knew that his wife was writing to various friends of hers, and was calling on them after dark. Why? She was keeping him in food by her lace work—sold doilies and tray cloths and made her friends who bought them swear they wouldn't tell. Walter Lister Glynne would have died of shame if he had known. Naturally, all this selling entailed a lot of correspondence and canvassing, and this poor simpleton, being jealous as blazes, thought that scattered round the country were a whole lot of compromising letters. He burgled one house after another, trying to find evidence of her flightiness—why, the Lord knows! Anyway, she's left him, and she is starting a little business in the West End. Some mug is lending her five hundred pounds for stock."

The superintendent thought he knew who that mug was.

CASE III

THE INHERITOR

CASE III

ANY country is a pretty small place for a man who wishes to avoid recognition. There were once two young men who worked together as student apprentices in a large drug store in the Midlands. In those days they were called "chemist shops," and the proprietor usually lived upstairs and kept his own books.

The two young men might have served as models for story-book characters of a more modern kind, for one was idle and honest, and the other was industrious and enterprising. The idle and honest apprentice married the daughter of his bankrupt master (she subsequently ran away from him), and eventually he became an habitual drunkard; the industrious apprentice was discharged at a minute's notice and left, taking with him a considerable sum of money and an odd assortment of pharmaceutic knowledge.

One day the drunkard, who had migrated to

London, saw a man step from a handsome
limousine, and accosted him by his name.

"Go to the devil!" said his wealthy fellow
apprentice.

Enraged by this reception, the down-and-out
struck at his old friend; a policeman intervened,
and a vulgar brawl might have ended in a police-
court conviction but for the fact that the prose-
cutor did not arrive to charge his assailant.

The man was released; a mysterious somebody sent him an envelope containing fifty
pounds in notes, and there would have been the
end of the matter but for the aggrieved prisoner,
under the influence of further libations, attend-
ing at Scotland Yard and demanding that the
name and address of his enemy should be given
to him. Nor would he leave until he had made
a most libellous statement concerning his former
companion, and this statement he insisted upon
reducing to writing.

Such things happen at Scotland Yard. Horrific
tales arrive daily, are probed with infinite pains
and patience and usually dispersed. The scope
for inquiry here was small; the document was
filed away in the "crazy drawer" and was forgotten. It concerned one Paul Sipbett, who had a
weakness for experiment.

Peter Dunn, hunting for a similar document one day, came upon it and wondered what was Amotoxylene (he gathered from the ill-written paper that this was the word), but he made no steps to discover its properties. As for the story of the wanton experiments on dogs, that was possible, but not worth further inquiry.

Old Superintendent Brissen used to say that all events were triplets: that if a red-haired man was arrested for burgling a fish shop, two other red-haired men would also be arrested for burgling fish shops.

He was mainly right, though Peter Dunn had never met coincidence eye to eye until he undertook the Bletsall inquiry.

First of all was the strange affair of the drunken man. It was odd in itself that this should have happened within twenty-four hours of his becoming acquainted with the story of the two apprentices.

Going back to his house that night, he found a man hanging onto the railings. He was in evening dress, apparently a gentleman, so far as a man can be a gentleman who permits himself the weakness of inebriation.

Peter would have passed him by, not because he was pharisaical, but because drunken people bored him, but the helpless young man spoke:

"I say—take my hands away, will you?"

His voice was thick and tremulous.

Peter halted.

"What's the matter with your hands?" he demanded.

"Can't let go."

The detective stepped to his side and tried to loosen the hands: they were gripped convulsively; it took all his strength to release them.

But for his arm, the victim would have fallen. It was as he supported the limp figure that he realized that certain symptoms of drunkenness were entirely absent. His house was near, and he half dragged and half carried the man into his study and dropped him onto a settee. It was half an hour before the wilted figure sat up of his own volition. He was deadly pale, sweat beads stood on his forehead and cheeks, and his eyes were strangely dilated until they were all pupils.

"Terribly sorry—I don't know what happened. Can't remember a darned thing!"

Peter had given him brandy, straight, and the spirit had been efficacious.

"No, I'm not tight. Awfully good of you to do this for me. I've not been very well all day—headache; took an aspirin——"

His name was Martin. Peter gathered that he had been in the army. He declined the invitation to be seen home and was well enough to walk to the cab which Peter called.

The second leg of the coincidence appeared a week later.

The life of a detective would be one grand sweet song if mysterious bank robberies and picturesque murders made up the round of his daily life. In reality his work is dull and wearisome. He spends his days and nights asking Bill Jones what has happened to his friend Harry Smith, and listening incredulously while Bill explains that the last time he saw Harry was two years ago come Easter.

Or else he is plodding on the clue of a laundry mark discovered on the shirt of a drowned man, or he is investigating the circumstances in which a ton of old lead piping disappears from a lock-up store under a railway arch and miraculously reappears in the back yard of a marine store dealer.

Sometimes, when work was very heavy and the leave season was in full swing, Peter Dunn took on odd little jobs for the Yard. He never despised odd jobs: they sometimes had curious and fascinating ramifications.

He reported for duty—he was relieving two men who were on their holidays—and found three jobs awaiting him. The first was an identification, which was soon disposed of, since the prisoner was at Cannon Row; the second a matter of a driving license which had been loaned by its confiding owner to a gentleman whose license had been suspended for a year for driving to the common danger; and the third was a petty cash affair in the office of Mr. Greeley Bletsall.

There was a man at Scotland Yard who knew everybody. He was a walking reference book, though his information could hardly have been published without involving him in innumerable suits for libel.

"Who is Bletsall? He's the big noise of the Greeley Trading Company. He's supposed to be worth a million, but he's been going badly on the Stock Exchange lately—he's the biggest mug punter the City has met for years. Owes money left and right——"

"Is he broke?"

The little inspector who was the source of information shook his untidy head. He was one of the dwindling army of snuff takers, as his soiled tunic proved.

"No; that kind of fellow isn't broke as we understand being broke—they don't have to count up the shillings on Saturdays. He owes a hundred thousand here and a hundred thousand there—that's high finance! He's had a lot of trouble in turning aside a couple of petitions."

2

Mr. Greeley Bletsall occupied a suite in St. James's Street, where he directed the affairs of a colonial trading company. The Greeley Trading Company was not a familiar name to the average Londoner who passed its office daily, but it had a magical sound to millions of uncultured natives who exchanged their rubber for Manchester goods and Birmingham brassware.

There was not a man or woman who lived on the Coast or in the dark interior of the Continent who did not know Greeley's.

Miss Henrietta Greeley had married Mr. Bletsall, who had been a young married clerk in the concern. On the death of his wife he had married the unprepossessing daughter of old Tom Greeley and had changed his name to Greeley Bletsall. When his wife had died on a sea voyage, he inherited the control of a company which was reputed to have a turnover of considerably more

than a million and a half a year. He had been in
Parliament, was on two insurance boards, be-
longed to certain exclusive clubs, and was famous
for his large gifts to charitable institutions.

Charitable as he was, he could not extend his
charity to the miscreant who had opened his
desk drawer and taken therefrom seven one-
pound notes.

"It is not the first time this has happened," he
told Peter. "I have missed money before. I
usually keep a number of notes in this drawer,
and I invariably keep a check on them by putting
in a slip of paper representing the amount I take
out."

It was a large and imposing desk in a large
and imposing room, panelled with walnut and
nobly furnished. Mr. Greeley Bletsall was himself on the large side—a big, sandy-haired man,
with a long, narrow face and pale blue eyes
which at the moment were gleaming wrathfully
under the shaggy eyebrows.

His polished table was a model of neatness,
innocent of litter, and he himself was as spotless
as his surroundings. There was no speck of
cigarette ash on his immaculate black coat to
testify to his human weakness.

He sat back in his padded chair, the fingertips

of one hand (exquisitely manicured, Peter noticed) touching the fingertips of the other. It was a prayerful gesture to be found on the tombs of old Crusaders, but Mr. Greeley Bletsall was not praying.

"There are three people I suspect: the porter" —he ticked them off daintily—"the office boy, and the young lady who assists my secretary. Just one moment."

He pressed an ivory bell push, and a girl came in. She was extraordinarily pretty, but just a little too pale, Peter thought. She had the cultured voice of a lady, but he detected in her some curious, unexpected nervousness—unexpected because he could not imagine that the confidential secretary of so important a man could be in the slightest degree uncomfortable in the presence of an officer of Scotland Yard.

"Miss Lane will tell you all she knows." Mr. Bletsall was impressive and a little pompous.

"I am afraid I don't know very much." She smiled faintly. "I came in yesterday morning and found the drawer unlocked. Somebody had used a key to open the drawer, but was unable to pull the key out after the drawer was open. I didn't miss the money, naturally, because I didn't know how much was there."

"You have the key," said Mr. Bletsall.

She went out to find it. It had been extracted with great difficulty by a locksmith.

"I suppose you have no doubt about Miss Lane?" said Peter.

It was a very commonplace question, and one he would have made in any circumstances, for it was his experience that even quite beautiful young ladies can pilfer their employers' desks.

The effect of this innocent inquiry upon Mr. Bletsall was amazing. His sallow face flushed red, he sat bolt upright in his chair, and the pale blue eyes blazed wrathfully.

"How dare you, sir!" His voice trembled. "Accuse my secretary! It is a monstrous suggestion. Miss Lane is incapable——"

"I merely asked." Peter hastened to appease the angry man.

"Miss Lane is a lady of the highest possible character, though in certain respects she may be a little wayward, but that is a privilege of youth."

At this moment the lady under discussion returned and put a little key on the desk. Peter was not greatly interested: it was a very common experience for a desk drawer to be opened by a key which was never intended to open it and for that key to "stick." He picked it up and examined it perfunctorily, then put it down again.

"You will not be able to trace the thief by that," he said. "It is a very ordinary type of key. There must be dozens of them in every City office. If you will give me a room I will question the people you suspect."

"Will it be necessary for me to charge them?" asked Mr. Bletsall. "I am a very busy man, and I have important duties which take up all my time."

"I haven't found the thief yet, sir," smiled Peter good-humouredly. "If I do, you will certainly have to charge him, or you can arrange for your secretary to appear——"

"Miss Lane will not appear in any police court," said Mr. Bletsall loudly. "I would sooner go myself a hundred times than submit that lady to the ignominy of—er——"

"I know what you mean," said Peter.

He was secretly amused and a little puzzled. The colour which came to the girl's pale face was certainly not caused by pleasure at this exhibition of her employer's solicitude. It spoke of embarrassment, possibly annoyance.

"I will show you into the waiting room," she

said, and turned and walked quickly into the outer office.

Peter followed.

3

She opened the door of the waiting room and came in after him, closing the door behind her.

"Mr. Dunn," she said a little breathlessly, "I am terribly afraid it *is* the porter. He has a sick wife, and he has had a lot of trouble with money-lenders. I have not dared tell Mr. Bletsall, for fear he would discharge him or something worse."

"Is the man here?"

She shook her head.

"He is away to-day—Mr. Bletsall doesn't even know that. I don't think you could prove it. I am quite willing to find the money myself to prevent a prosecution."

Peter pursed his lips thoughtfully.

"I don't know exactly what I can do in the matter. You'd better fix it with Mr. Bletsall. I am sure he would do the reasonable thing if you asked him," he said.

This was no novel situation: it was one with which the police are frequently confronted. They are always reluctant to bring a first of-

fender in the court, and will even condone petty
larceny to avoid the ruin of a man's career.

She looked at him thoughtfully.

"No," she said, with a little catch in her
breath. "I don't want to be under any—I don't
wish to ask Mr. Bletsall. Couldn't you speak
for him? I'd much rather you did."

There was no mystery here either. Evidently
there were many reasons why she did not wish
to be under an obligation to her employer—Peter
guessed one.

"I will see the porter," he said, "if you give
me his address. Has he confessed to you that he
has stolen the money?"

She hesitated.

"No," she said at last, but he didn't believe
her.

"I've asked somebody to see Jansen this morning," she said. "A friend of mine—which was
selfish of me, for he has been terribly ill. I am
afraid there is little he can do."

Jansen, the porter, lived in a workman's flat
near Notting Hill, a tired, middle-aged man, who
almost fainted when Peter revealed his identity.

"Come in, sir," he faltered at last. "Miss
Lane's young gentleman is here. He came to see

if he could fix things up for me. My wife has just been taken to hospital. Thank God she doesn't know anything about this business."

Here was a pitiful little tragedy the like of which Peter had seen again and again: a man with a blameless record who had succumbed to temptation and stolen a few pounds. Such as he come in endless procession to the police courts of the land, some to pass under probation, some to prison and a subsequent criminal career.

Peter followed him to the poorly furnished little parlour. The young man, who was standing by the window and looking into the street, turned as they came in. He was young, rather good-looking, the type which public schools turn out by the thousand.

For a second Peter did not know the visitor, though he could guess that this was Miss Lane's young gentleman.

And then, suddenly, he recognized him.

"Hello! Better?"

Mr. Martin was momentarily puzzled.

"Good Lord! You are the fellow who was so decent to me the other night."

They shook hands.

"Yes, I'm well enough, though I felt pretty bad for a few days. You've come to see Jansen?"

The detective explained his business in a few words, and the trembling porter sank into a chair, incapable of speech.

"Yes, I took the money, sir; I thought I would be able to put it back. It was not seven pounds—it was three, and the last time it was one. I have been twenty years in the office, sir, and I was with old Mr. Greeley when he died. I was the last person to see him alive—took in an aspirin, and I'd hardly got out of the office before he was dead. Heart trouble, like his poor daughter suffered from."

Peter looked at him long and thoughtfully.

"Oh, indeed. Now tell me about this theft of yours."

"Mr. Bletsall sent you, sir? He was good to me in those days: he sent me abroad to Africa to collect Mr. Greeley's papers when he died and gave me fifty pounds. I ought to be ashamed of what I've done."

He hid his head in his arms and began to sob.

"It was not the only thing I took. I might as well make a clean breast of it. I was not sure which drawer the money was in, so I opened the bottom one first, took out a case, and put it in my pocket. He sometimes keeps his money in the pocket case. I locked the drawer and was going away when I found I had made a mistake, and tried the second drawer; that's where the key stuck."

"Where is the pocket case?" asked Peter.

Without a word the man went out of the room and came back with a flat leather case. Peter opened it and examined its contents before he slipped it in his pocket. Then Jansen broke down again, and Peter beckoned the young man out of the room.

"I am afraid there is not much to be done," he said. "I shall have to take a statement from him, and Bletsall must prosecute."

"It's a damnable shame," said the young man hotly. "Bletsall has underpaid him for years."

"You know Mr. Bletsall?"

"Yes, slightly. I know Miss Lane better."

"You are her young gentleman, in fact," said Peter, with a twinkle in his eye.

The young man smiled ruefully.

"Yes. We are engaged. She asked me to call on this chap this morning and see if I could do anything for him. If Bletsall sets his mind on prosecuting, he will prosecute. He is a vindictive beast; though, perhaps, I ought not to say that: he offered me a very good job to take charge of one of his stations in Africa."

There was something in his voice which made Peter look at him keenly.

"You have turned it down, haven't you?"

"Yes, I have turned it down," said the other. He hesitated. "I cannot afford to, but—well, I'd rather be in London for all sorts of reasons."

Peter interviewed the broken man again. Obviously he was incapable of making any statement at the moment, and Peter decided to go back to St. James's Street.

Here he had a surprise: Mr. Bletsall's attitude was entirely changed.

"Very stupid of me, Inspector——"

"Sergeant," murmured Peter.

"Sergeant, is it? Well, the truth is that I told this man to take any money he wanted out of my desk."

"He's an old servant of the family, isn't he?" asked Peter.

"He has been here some years," agreed Mr. Bletsall, in his stateliest manner.

Peter nodded.

"So he said."

He fastened his notebook and put it into his pocket.

"So we shall let the matter rest, shall we, Mr. Bletsall?"

"If you please."

He put his hand in his pocket rather ostentatiously.

"If you are going to offer me a reward, I'll save
you the trouble," said Peter, smiling. "I must
report the matter to headquarters, but I don't
suppose they will take any further action."

He had noticed, as he came into the office, the
little glass box which served Miss Lane as an
office. He knocked at the door and went in.

She was sitting at her desk, but she was not
working. She turned with a look of alarm on her
face, which cleared as she saw the visitor.

"We fixed Jansen," he said. "I thought you
would like to know."

Obviously it was no news to her.

"Yes, I know. Did you meet Mr. Martin?"

He was still standing at the door, and from
here he commanded a private view of the glass-
panelled door which led to Bletsall's office. He
saw the shadow of the man against the glass
panel.

"Yes." Then, lowering his voice: "Do you go
out to tea?"

He was amused at the sudden doubt which
came into her eyes, and grinned.

"No, I am not being gallant," he said, "but I

am trying to make a date with you. Do you think you could meet me at—" he named a fashionable tea shop near at hand—"at five o'clock?"

She hesitated, and then he heard Bletsall's voice addressing him in the corridor.

"Yes," she said, and he came out to meet the big man's suspicious scrutiny.

"I thought I would tell Miss Lane that the matter had been settled," he said.

"It was not necessary," snapped Bletsall.

4

Once outside the office, Peter hailed a taxicab and a few minutes later was interviewing his chief at Scotland Yard. It was a long interview, because the heads of departments were called in; there were visits to the Record Office, and a hastily summoned analyst made rapid experiments in his laboratory.

It was a quarter of an hour after the appointed time that Miss Lane came hurrying into the tea room; she was breathlessly apologetic.

"It was difficult to get away," she said, "but fortunately Mr. Bletsall was called to the City."

He found a quiet corner of the room and ordered tea.

"You know I am a detective?"

"I know all about you." In spite of her trouble, she could smile. "You are Sir Peter Dunn. Mr. Bletsall doesn't know, but I was reading something about you in the newspapers, and I recognized your photograph."

"I shall have to raise the salary of my publicity agent." Then he went on seriously: "You know I am a detective, and I am going to ask you a few questions for my own private information." Then he asked her: "Has this man been making love to you?"

She changed colour and seemed inclined for a moment to resent his blunt methods.

"Yes; Mr. Bletsall has asked me to marry him."

"You are engaged to Martin, aren't you?"

She nodded.

"Bletsall has offered him a post at a thousand a year in Africa."

He saw her lips curl.

"At Maleti! It is built on a swamp. Four of the agents have died there in three years."

"When was the offer made?"

"About a week ago. Mr. Bletsall took Ivor out to dinner and put the offer before him. He didn't tell me that he was taking Ivor; it was done very secretly. Fortunately I told Ivor about Maleti. It is a horrid position for me: he pays me a very big salary. I simply can't afford to leave, because my young sister is at school——"

Peter was putting sugar into a fresh cup of tea when he saw her look up with an expression of alarm. Mr. Bletsall was standing a few yards away, glowering down at them, and he came slowly forward.

"I thought you were at the office, Miss Lane," he said coldly.

The girl was obviously terrified of him. She rose without a word of apology and slipped past him out of the shop. For a few seconds he stood staring at the detective.

"Sit down, Mr. Bletsall."

To Peter's surprise, the big man came slowly to the table, drew up a chair, and sat down.

"This is hardly part of your duty, is it? Or is it pleasure?"

"Purely pleasure," said Peter. "I was discussing the future of Jansen."

"There is no need to discuss the future of Jansen—that is assured," said Bletsall.

Peter looked at him for a second, and then:

"Why didn't you prosecute the fellow who struck you about three months ago in Regent Street?"

The colour went from the man's face, then slowly faded back again.

"Because I didn't choose," he said.

His attitude was frankly antagonistic, but he must have had the most amazing command over his emotions, for suddenly he laughed.

"Mr. Dunn," he said, "you understand that my position is rather a peculiar one. Money is very tight in the City. I have been having heavy losses, and I could not afford to figure in a vulgar brawl. If it happened to-day I wouldn't mind, because I have made a great deal of money, and I could afford to snap my fingers at my enemies."

He lowered his voice.

"I suppose you realize that there is a financial combination in the City of London which has been doing its best to ruin me for five years?"

He was obviously sincere. Rapidly he named the heads of three great finance corporations, familiar figures in the City, and men whose integrity was a household word.

"Don't let's beat about the bush, Mr. Dunn. I know you came to inquire into the robbery, but the real reason for your inquiries was to discover my financial position."

Peter shook his head.

"Police officers do not——" he began, but the other interrupted him.

"I did not expect you to admit it," he smiled. "Well, you can tell your friends that by Wednesday morning their accounts will be cleared, and I shall have a million to my credit at the Bank of England—that should satisfy them. Luck has always been on my side," he went on gaily. "I am an inheritor. If my big deal hadn't come off, somebody would have died and left me a million."

"That's very interesting," said Peter. He did not remove his gaze from the pale blue eyes. "I know several other people who would like to hear all about your good fortune."

"Finish up your tea and we'll go," said Mr. Bletsall, pushing back his chair.

Peter took one sip and dropped the cup with a crash onto the table. In another second he had gripped Bletsall by the arm.

"Don't be absurd," said Mr. Bletsall.

All the way to Scotland Yard he was babbling of the cars he had bought, of the magnificent estate for which he was negotiating, and the millions which would be his in the very near future.

5

Even a sip of diluted amotoxylene was sufficient to send Peter to bed, gripping the sheets convulsively. Superintendent Brissen came round to see him in the morning.

"Shan't be able to do very much with that bird," he said. "He's a killer from his youth up. He's got two dead wives and old Greeley to his credit, and Heaven knows how many other people. He must have discovered the loss of the little medicine case that Jansen stole. There was enough poison there to kill a regiment of soldiers. Martin probably only had a small dose, but he must have dropped three or four pellets into your tea when you weren't looking. Detectives are certainly difficult to kill."

"Good detectives are," said Peter.

CASE IV

DR. FIFER'S PATIENT

CASE IV

DR. FIFER'S PATIENT

"Yours, sir, must be an interesting profession," said Skipper.

He invariably made some such fool remark, and Peter Dunn as invariably answered according to his folly.

One cannot be unkind to a butler, for butlers out of their native element are helpless creatures. Mr. Harrivay's butler, Skipper, who frequently came to Peter's house with urgent letters from his master, and sometimes from his mistress, was one of those men who might very easily be hurt. He was a large man, with a big, solemn face embellished with side whiskers, and he was talkative. That was the only black mark against him in Peter's book, for he was one of those incessant talkers whose conversation never showed a crack into which a wedge of interruption might be thrust.

Mainly he talked about his butler experiences in America.

"It's a country I never wish to go back to——"

"Yes, yes." Peter was a little impatient with the messenger that spring morning, for he was a busy man. "Take this note to Mrs. Harrivay."

Peter did not dislike Skipper—nobody disliked Skipper. He was one of those negative people entirely without personality who can be very exhausting to the objective mind.

He was one of Stanley's discoveries; he had been found penniless and dishevelled through the prosaic instrumentality of a Labour Exchange. Stanley got him cheap and was immensely proud of his find.

"The poor devil had been years in hospital and was down and out," he said.

Skipper would have died of starvation if he had had to live on the wages that Mr. Stanley Harrivay paid him.

Skipper repaid his employer with sleepless service and a devotion which Stanley, who was not original, described as doglike.

"Mr. Harrivay is well?" asked Peter politely, as he sealed the envelope.

"Extraordinarily well, sir," said Skipper gravely. "In the eighteen months I have had the honour of serving him I have never known

him to be so well. He had a slight cold in July.
I think it was on the 23rd that he began to
sneeze—it may have been the 24th——"

"I accept the 23rd," said Peter.

"Thank you, sir," said Skipper gratefully, and
bowed himself out.

Stanley Harrivay was a cousin of Peter Dunn
—a fact which he did not emphasize until Peter
inherited his title and a fortune. Mr. Harrivay
had not been without hope that the estrange-
ment between old man Dunn and his grandson
would be permanent. The title must, of course,
go to Peter, but the big money could be willed
anywhere—and why not to himself, who, next
to Peter, was in the direct line of succession?

Peter became a common policeman, which was
rather low of him, as Mr. Stanley Harrivay said
in the course of a letter to his elderly relative.
Until this rash act Stanley had been quite
friendly with Peter, had sent him solid presents
on his birthday; Peter had spent week-ends at
Felbourne Manor and at least one Christmas
week.

Mr. Harrivay was comfortably circumstanced.
He was, in truth, a fairly rich man, but fairly
rich men are usually ambitious to be very rich
men, and the possibility of the Dunn million

coming his way brought about a considerable change in Mr. Harrivay's attitude toward his cousin.

And when "that fellow Peter" became "Sir Peter," and it was discovered that he had taken with the title all the worldly possessions of his grandfather, Mr. Harrivay was not only surprised but deeply hurt.

Nevertheless, his was the first letter congratulating the heir upon his fortune.

"After all," said Mr. Harrivay to his wife, "Peter is the kind of fellow who may never marry; I am his nearest relation and—well, you never know what might happen."

So Peter was invited again to Felbourne Manor, which was near High Barnet, to spend his week-ends. And Peter replied politely that he would be delighted to come, but unfortunately he was on duty during the week-end—in fact, during all week-ends.

He was invited for Ascot week—the Harrivays had a box. Peter replied that it was a tragedy that he was on duty during the Ascot week.

Mr. Harrivay, who was not easily daunted, asked him to lunch with him at the Carlton, and Peter accepted this compromise.

2

Peter did not like Stanley Harrivay, who was a thin, querulous man, sandy and bald. He did not like his big feet, or his knock-knees, or his habit of quarrelling with waiters and sending dishes back to the chef because they weren't cooked to his liking.

Peter did like Mrs. Harrivay, who was younger and prettier than her husband, and who, in the days of Peter's disgrace, had sent him nice letters and an offer of a secret allowance. Stanley never knew that they had lunched together with great frequency, and that Peter was the repository of her confidences.

Skipper, the butler, had that day brought an urgent note from Stella. She wished to see Peter, and would call at his house in Berkeley Square for tea.

Peter disentangled himself from an important conference he was to have attended at Scotland Yard and hurried home to meet her.

The afternoon post had brought him a very correctly worded invitation from his cousin to spend the week-end at Felbourne.

"I want you to meet a very interesting fellow —an American doctor," wrote Stanley, and went

on to describe the qualities and peculiar attrac-
tions of his guest.

Peter had already invented his excuses when
he reached home to find his pretty relative awaiting him.

He had a shock when he saw her: she looked
tired and drawn.

"No, I haven't been sleeping well. I wanted to
see you about that. I mean the cause, but it is
so silly that I don't think I will. Has Stanley
asked you to Felbourne for the week-end? Don't
come! It will worry me to know that there is
another bored person in the house besides me.
One of Stanley's odd friends will be staying with
us—a doctor he met in New York last summer."

"A psychiatrist?" Peter consulted the letter
of invitation. "Stanley says he is an authority
on crime—that put me off."

She nodded.

"We met him in town last week. He is a Dr.
Fifer——"

"Fifer? Not Cornelius Fifer? Good Lord!"
Peter looked at the letter again. "He didn't
mention the name. Yes, I know Fifer very well
by repute. I am lunching with him to-morrow;
he is in charge of a criminal lunatic institution
somewhere in America."

Stella made a little face.

"It is going to be a horrible week-end," she said. "Dr. Fifer is bringing down his photographic albums—you know how morbidly interested Stanley is in these dreadful things."

"I wonder whether Stanley interests Dr. Fifer as a psychiatrist or as an individual?"

She smiled faintly at this.

"That's not very kind; you know Stanley—he does manage to impress scientists. He took up the study of criminology after he lost his interest in the breeding of Angora rabbits."

She would have changed the conversation, but he detected something odd in her tone, in the very abruptness with which she turned to another topic, and questioned her.

"Well——" She hesitated. "I *am* nervy. I had a horrid experience last night. Perhaps Stanley thinks I am mad, too. I really came to ask your advice."

She had heard movements in her room and had wakened in time to see a blurred silhouette against the moonlit corridor.

"Stanley," suggested Peter, but she shook her head.

"He sleeps in the next room. Stanley snores dreadfully. I could hear him through the wall.

It must have been a burglar. I found my handbag on the floor. It was open."

"Nothing gone?"

"Nothing—— At least, only Dr. Fifer's letter which Stanley had given me and which I had put in my bag. A burglar would hardly break into one's house to steal a letter. I screamed; it did not wake Stanley, but it frightened the burglar. Skipper heard me and came down. He wanted to wake Stanley, but I wouldn't have that. It was Skipper who found the handbag on the floor near the bed."

"Can anybody get admission to the house?" asked Peter. "I mean, any of the servants who sleep outside?"

She thought for a moment.

"I'd forgotten that. Yes—the chauffeur. He is not a good chauffeur, but Stanley knew his grandfather. You know how odd Stanley is in choosing servants."

Peter thought quickly.

"I will come down on Saturday morning," he said, "unless this fellow bores me at lunch, in which case I won't come down at all."

3

But Dr. Fifer did not bore Peter. He was a tall, gaunt man, and his beard was more grey than black. He was an easy man to entertain, for he talked most of the time and was only content to listen when Peter described the methods of Scotland Yard.

"You have no psychiatrist? Well, I should not like to say you are wrong. A lot of psychiatry is bunk. You can't always get the mental slants of convicts by making them draw squares and triangles and by getting them to find their way out of a picture maze. You can get them by listening to them, encouraging them to talk, kidding their vanities—and they have got plenty of them. Take poisoners——"

Peter smiled.

"I am the last authority on the mind of the poisoner," he said, and told the doctor the story of Mr. Greeley Bletsall, which was his last big case.

Dr. Fifer listened keenly, keeping up a rapid fire of questions.

"Humph! I can go one worse than that! By the way, you will have another poison case in your hands; they run in twos. Gas suicides run in fours, crimes of jealousy in threes. It's odd, but there it is. There is a law governing such things. I had a man in my institution who poisoned his mother-in-law, his wife, the family doctor, and a United States sheriff. He was a fellow named Roanby—an Englishman. He was turned over to an institution in Massachusetts after I had him a year. By no test was he mad. In fact, I was the only psychiatrist who gave evidence on his behalf—I saved him from the death penalty. Poisoners, as a rule, are the sanest murderers that ever come before a judge— I believe this fellow was mad. He was my pet patient, and I hated like hell losing him. Ingenious? He was diabolically clever! In one of the murders he used whisky—wood alcohol stuff. Naturally, the coroner said 'misadventure.'"

Peter looked forward to meeting the psychiatrist during the week-end. He was fated to see Dr. Fifer—but not alive.

Dr. Fifer arrived on the Friday afternoon at Felbourne Manor, and he was not in the best of tempers; when taking his overcoat and suitcase from the car in which he arrived, Skipper dropped the doctor's glasses on the ground and smashed them, and without his glasses the doctor was a blind man.

"I never wear them when I am travelling," he snapped (Stanley was trying to suggest methods by which the misfortune might have been avoided). "I sleep in cars: only idiots look at

scenery. If your servant had not been the biggest
fool—— However, it doesn't matter; I can get
a pair from my hotel. How they fell out is a
mystery. I have a special pocket for my glasses."

The spare pair arrived by special messenger
after dinner, and with them the messenger
brought a number of letters which had arrived
by the mail. It was after reading these that Dr.
Fifer's manner changed; he scarcely spoke,
seemed to Stella to grow nervous. He asked
Stanley Harrivay if it was possible to telephone
to Boston, and if there was a telephone in his
bedroom (there was, in point of fact, an ex-
tension). At ten o'clock that night his call came
through. From that hour he did not leave his
room, the door of which he had locked, except
to come out for a few minutes and bawl a good-
night in his old manner, before he retired for the
night.

His bedroom was next to Stanley's, who heard
him moving about; heard him again at half-past
seven the next morning. Each room at Felbourne
Manor had a bathroom attached. Two bath-
rooms, those of Stanley and the doctor, had a
communicating door, which was locked and
bolted on both sides.

Stanley heard Fifer "pottering about," as he

subsequently put it, in the bathroom, and a little later the click of the lock turning. Stanley shouted "Good-morning" through the closed door. He heard the doctor growl something and then:

"How do you turn this faucet?"

It was then that the host remembered that the cold-water tap in the wash basin was out of order. If you knew the trick of it, it was easy to turn. Stanley bawled his instructions through the door. Apparently the doctor tried to turn on the cold water, but unsuccessfully.

"All right, all right," he boomed testily. "I am taking a bath, so it doesn't matter."

Stanley heard the bath taps turned off, and then the clink of glass against glass. Almost immediately after he heard a roar of pain and the thud of a heavy body falling. He tried to get through into the bathroom, but the door was bolted. Flying out of his room, he made an unsuccessful attempt to get in through the doctor's bedroom. Not only that, but the bathroom was locked. It was a quarter of an hour before the doors were broken open and Dr. Fifer's dead body was discovered.

The news came through to the Yard while Peter was in his office, and he was the first to

jump from the police car when it drew up under
the portico of Felbourne Manor. Stella was
waiting to receive him, for he had phoned her
that he was coming. He expected to find her
hysterical, but she was calm, and her voice was
steady. She alone of the household was able to
give a coherent account of what had occurred.

Stanley, who had made his appearance almost
immediately, was in a pitiable state of collapse.

"It's a terrible thing to have happened. Such
a clever man. I'm sure it is suicide. Has Stella
told you? My God, it's awful!"

It was some time before Peter could get Stella
alone, and then he heard as much of the story as
she could tell.

He went upstairs and saw the unfortunate
man. He was lying on the bed and was still
wearing his pajamas. The police surgeon who had
examined him took Peter by the arm and led
him outside.

"If this isn't a case of cyanide poisoning, I've
never seen one," said the surgeon. "I should
think it's a very ordinary suicide, but we'll be
able to tell accurately the cause of death in a
few days."

Peter returned to the bedroom. It was a big
apartment, comfortably furnished, and leading

out was the bathroom, where the body had been found. On a table were laid out the dead man's shaving kit and such articles of toilet, hairbrush, comb, etc., as he might require. The detectives who had searched the room had not found any sign of poison. There was a water bottle on a glass shelf. It was three parts full, and over it was an inverted glass.

When the bathroom door had been forced the cold-water faucet in the wash basin was running.

"We found this," said the divisional inspector, who came in while Peter was examining the room. "It was in the pocket of his dressing gown, which was hanging up behind the door."

"This" was an automatic pistol, the magazine of which contained nine cartridges, the tenth being in the chamber.

"The safety catch isn't up. It looks as though he was expecting to use it at any moment. Here are some papers we found in the waste-paper basket."

The "papers" were cable forms. On each had been written an address, "Saline Boston," and a few words of an unfinished message.

The first ran:

"In case cannot reach you by phone want you check up Walter Roanby . . ."

The second began:

"*Check whereabouts Roanby English poisoner transferred 1926 . . .*"

The third was illegible, for the words had been erased.

On the dressing table were the letters the dead man had received the night before, and Peter read them through. To his surprise they were business letters, none of which contained the least excuse for the perturbation which the doctor had shown after reading.

4

Peter went into the bathroom and examined every object carefully. If the man had committed suicide it was certain he would find the bottle or carton which had contained the poison. Even if it had been in pellet shape, it would have had some wrapping. There was nothing of this character. He went down to the servants' quarters and interviewed Skipper.

"No, sir; no servant went to his bedroom this morning. He did not have morning tea or anything else. In fact, he told the mistress he did not require it."

After the body had been removed, Peter made another search of the room. Who was Walter Roanby? The English poisoner who was transferred to—Massachusetts!

It was at that moment that Peter connected the dead man's reminiscences with the murder. But evidently the cables had been begun before the telephone message from Boston came through.

Peter decided to speak to Boston himself, and in the meantime put an inquiry through to London. And while he was examining the room he was called by the transatlantic service, who gave him the Boston number that the doctor had asked for on the previous night.

Peter looked at his watch: it was eleven o'clock—that would be six o'clock in the morning in Boston, and the line would be fairly clear. He repeated the number and made an urgent request for immediate connection. While he was waiting for this he continued his search, and re-read the letters that had come by the messenger from London. They were very ordinary business letters, that from America being about the doctor's new book, and requesting an elucidation of some passage which was not clear to the printer's reader.

He went into the bathroom and again inspected its contents. The inverted glass over the water bottle interested him. He felt the inside—it was quite dry. The communicating door between the doctor's bathroom and Stanley's had been unlocked, and he passed through. The toilet furnishings were identical. There was the the same glass and the same bottle, but, unlike the bottle in the doctor's bathroom, this one was full, and the inverted glass was wet. There were drops of water on the outside of the bottle where it had drained.

He went out into the corridor and called Stanley.

"Yes, I opened the communicating door. I unlocked my side and pushed the bolt back when I heard him fall. When I found him dead I unlocked his side of the door."

"You haven't taken any water out of this bottle this morning?"

Stanley shook his head.

Peter poured out a little drop of water from the doctor's bottle, put his finger in, and tasted it. There was neither the smell nor the taste of cyanide, and the rough test made of the water which had been sent to the analyst brought him no nearer to the solution of the mystery, nor did he expect to find that the water was poisoned. He was still looking at the bottle when the telephone bell rang and, after a delay of a minute, a sleepy voice demanded his business in a strong American accent.

By great luck he had reached the one man to whom he wished to speak, and the nine minutes' conversation he had was very illuminating.

Walter Roanby had escaped from the institution two years before and had disappeared.

"The doctor was mad at us for not letting him know, but he has been travelling for two years— he went to China and India—and I guess he did not read any American newspapers. Yes, Roanby escaped—rode the train out of Boston to Philadelphia. He was seen there and chased by a Yard cop. Went West, I believe; we've heard no more about him since."

Peter asked a number of questions, only a few of which the institute superintendent could answer.

"Clever? I should say he was! He escaped by drugging the guard: he got the drug out of the dispensary by soaking the corner of his handkerchief in morphine every time he came to the drug store, and collected it drop by drop."

Peter had the doctor's overcoat brought to him. In one of the big side pockets he found the spectacle case containing the smashed glasses. The case itself was crushed and mud-stained and bore the heel mark of the clumsy butler. Searching, Peter found the place into which the case usually fitted. It was a narrow pocket on the left breast of the coat, and when Peter pushed in the flattened case, he found that it fitted tightly.

Stanley Harrivay as a witness was entirely useless, and it was to Stella that Peter turned for information.

"Do you remember discussing the doctor at dinner the evening before you came to see me?" he asked.

There had been such a discussion, she said.

"Did you mention him by name?"

Here she was able to give him an emphatic answer.

"No. Stanley has an exasperating memory for names and could not tell me—he had left the doctor's letter upstairs in his room and brought it downstairs just as I was going to bed, and I put it into my bag—it was rather a long letter, and I wasn't terribly interested, but didn't want to hurt Stanley's feelings by skimming it in front of him."

That evening Peter went to the local station and had a long conference with the divisional inspector and the police surgeon.

At a quarter to seven, when Skipper was laying the table, he found the room suddenly filled with complete strangers. He made a fight, but not the fight he intended, because his hand was never left free to pull the gun he carried.

"It was the toothbrush that put me on the track," explained Peter to his superior. "It was wet, and there was no reason why it should be wet; for the glass in which it should have been soaked was bone dry in spite of the fact that a glassful of water had been poured out of the bottle. Fifer couldn't turn the tap, or faucet as he called it. Yet it was running when Stanley noticed it—which was probably some time after the murder. Only a person acquainted with the cold-water tap could have turned it on—that person was Roanby, or Skipper, as he called himself. The peculiar fact I noticed was that although the brush was wet, there was no toothpaste, but there was the leaden screw-top of a paste tube. Somebody had removed the paste—the somebody who had washed the toothbrush. The poison was in the paste. We found the tube at the bottom of Skipper's trunk.

"It was one of the unlikely chances of life that brought Fifer to the house. Skipper knew him well and hated him, though Fifer had testified to the prisoner's insanity at his trial, and it was Fifer's evidence that had saved the man from

the chair. Skipper heard at dinner that a psychiatrist was coming, and, although the name was
never mentioned, he had a feeling that it was
Fifer. He saw Stanley Harrivay give a letter to
his wife, and went into her bedroom that night
to make absolutely sure that it was Fifer who
was coming.

"That he should regard the man who saved
his life as an enemy may seem odd to those who
do not understand a convict's attitude towards
those in authority. The doctor meant exposure
and, as Skipper believed, rearrest and extradition.

"Skipper had studied the doctor when he was
an inmate of the institution, and knew the doctor's sight was poor. Skipper told me that if
Fifer had recognized him he would have shot
him on the spot. He had already staged an accident and had taken out and loaded Stanley's
gun, and put it under the portico. But the doctor
was not wearing his glasses. Skipper snatched
the coat, jerked the glasses underfoot and broke
them. He had made so careful a study of the
doctor's habits that he knew exactly where the
glasses would be. Anyway, it saved an unpleasant
shooting accident.

"Unfortunately for Skipper, another pair of
glasses was available. When he realized the game
was up, he went upstairs, where he had laid out

the doctor's kit, and injected cyanide into his toothpaste with a hypodermic needle. He must have done this during the dinner.

"Apparently the doctor did not use paste on his teeth overnight. Even then Skipper hoped to escape recognition, but no sooner had Fifer put on his glasses than he recognized the man, though evidently he was not certain—hence the telephone message to Boston. But Fifer was moody and silent after that. Mr. and Mrs. Harrivay thought it was because he had had bad news in the letters. The real reason was that he was almost certain that he was sleeping under the same roof as a desperate murderer. He slept with a gun under his pillow that night. It was found in his dressing-gown pocket.

"The doctor could not turn on the tap, yet it was running. It was Skipper who, in the confusion following the discovery of the body, turned on the tap to wash the glass, and, passing through into Stanley's bathroom, substituted one for another."

Walter Roanby, *alias* Skipper, was hanged at Pentonville Gaol. He had no psychiatrist to testify to his insanity, for the only man who believed Skipper was mad was dead—had died at Skipper's own hands.

CASE V

THE BURGLAR ALARM

CASE V

THE BURGLAR ALARM

SUPERINTENDENT LEIGH of the Criminal Investigation Department was a difficult man to please. The best job of work earned no more from him than a grunt which had in it an unnecessary amount of disparagement. It was a legend that if Mr. Leigh ever expressed his pleasure and approbation it would be his last conscious utterance on earth.

He had never approved of Peter Dunn; but then, he had never approved of anybody. He told Peter he was a little too conspicuous in the Service, and said this many times.

"You're too confident, Sergeant, too infernally sure. I don't say you're any worse than any young officer, but, then, policemen are like that nowadays. The old brand of discreet officer is dying out—in fact, is almost dead."

Peter was sorry that it was not quite dead, but wisely he did not express this opinion.

Peter certainly was conspicuous. He had even excited the curiosity of Ann Kelski.

She learned of Peter from Mike Leary. As a

woman she was not unnaturally intrigued by the phenomenon of a titled policeman; as an artist she resented the respect with which her companion spoke of this officer.

"All cops are dumb," she said, and felt that experience justified her contempt. She was a little slangy at that period, for she had been playing around with Mike and the Stack gang, who were one hundred per centers and had their haunts in wholesome American cities, some of which would have been glad to entertain the remainder of their bodies in the state jail.

Ann felt superior to policemen just then, for she had lifted a million-mark pearl necklace from a store on Unter den Linden and had walked through a cordon of rubber-truncheoned policemen, with the pearls inside her neat little hat.

Heredity counted with Ann, who was the daughter of the best jewel thief on two continents; she was by birth British, European by education, wholly dangerous, completely without scruples, clever.

She came to London, spent three months at a fashionable hotel, then sent for Mike Leary to do a job which she had so carefully planned that even Mike, who was on the dumb side, could not possibly fall into error.

Peter Dunn stored in his head odd scraps of information concerning people, and the name of Ann Kelski was in a faint and elusive way oddly familiar. There are certain American publications which carry interesting articles on those criminals who operate exclusively on the Continent of Europe, and it was through this medium that he had made a fleeting acquaintance with the ingenious Ann.

There seemed little likelihood of his coming into personal contact with the "big shots" of the Continental underworld, for these ladies and gentlemen usually give Great Britain a wide berth. But he did meet Mike Leary.

"There's too much law in your damn country and too much sea around it."

Thus did Mike summarize the disadvantages of operating in England. And he said this in a moment of great bitterness and sincerity when, with handcuffs on his wrists and a strap about his ankles, he was being brought back from Dover by Peter Dunn to answer a charge of breaking into the Central Midland Bank. The strap was necessary, for Mike had made an attempt to leap from the window of the carriage in which he was travelling.

Mike made no reference to Ann Kelski; and

her name was not associated with the offense even when it was discovered that Mike carried none of the stolen property, which was remarkable, for the police had been hot on his scent. It was known that he had worked single-handed. He had been seen leaving the bank and had been chased. Peter, who had charge of the case, could account for almost every minute of the man's time, and there had been detectives on the boat train keeping him under observation, and every person who approached him or spoke to him had been detained at Dover and searched—everybody except the people who occupied the coupé at the end of the Pullman car. These were a middle-aged lady, accompanied by a gawky nurse girl carrying a baby. The nurse girl was questioned because Leary had stopped in the doorway to speak to the child.

But nobody had dreamed of searching the baby, and it was in the shawl which swathed it that some seventy thousand pounds' worth of negotiable bonds went to France.

2

Peter knew only this about Ann Kelski: that she was personable, was British by birth, and for three years had been an actress in Paris. She had no English domicile, and, save for his fleeting acquaintance with her in the American Press and the knowledge that she had served a term in a French prison, he had no exact knowledge of her. If a quarter-page drawing he had seen meant anything, she was beautiful; but drawings are apt to be deceptive when they are published in Sunday supplements, where all lady crooks are *ipso facto* beautiful.

Mike Leary went down to the shades with the philosophical fortitude which is part of the professional's equipment. He gave no information about the stolen property, though it was hinted to him that a squeal that recovered the money would make quite an appreciable difference to the length of his sentence.

It was natural that the newspapers should not forget that, though the robber had been convicted, the stolen money had not been found. A crime expert talked of a woman accomplice, and Peter very rashly expressed an opinion, which was printed:

"The clever woman bank robber is merely an imaginative character. Women are decoys, swindlers, larcenists, but they are not clever enough to undertake work of this description."

Peter made this statement after a very irritating interview with Mr. Leigh. It was a statement (said that officer) which no policeman should make in any circumstances, and when Peter read it in print he was aghast at his own indiscretion. He accepted the inevitable official reprimand for "improperly and without consulting his superiors making an unauthorized communication to the Press" with patience and good-humour.

But the biggest kick of all had yet to come. Ann Kelski read his views and quivered with annoyance; she was that much feminine.

Most of the things she said about Peter Dunn and the English police generally were unprintable, for she spoke worse languages than French, German, and English. Some great artists are touchy and morbidly sensitive about the quality of their work, and the mildest criticism is resented. Ann was one of these. And really Mr. Dunn had offered her an injustice, for she was a brilliant woman, and "ingenious" is a pale word to employ when describing tricks of hers which were as clever as any devised by a modern magician, and impersonations which certainly outshone the applauded efforts of real actresses; for it was she who so successfully faked a cheque for a million francs, and passed it at the Crédit Lyonnais under the eyes and with the apparent approval of a rich and elderly admirer, who had given her a cheque for ten thousand to buy a little present she desired. She had taken this near-sighted man to the bank, pushed the cheque to the teller, and, with the aid of a confederate who distracted the unhappy man's attention while the money was paid, walked out of the bank with her victim—and the money.

It was Ann Kelski who cleared the stock of a Viennese jeweller by a trick so simple that to describe it in detail would be against public policy.

"Peter Dunn—Sergeant Peter Dunn—say, what's the meaning of that 'Sir' in front of his name?"

Somebody explained the mystery of the baronetcy, but Ann Kelski was neither impressed nor interested, for titles meant nothing to her.

She took herself to Cannes and spent a week interviewing likely assistants for the task she had in hand.

"Leary was a bad break. Done? Not done, but dead! I'd have asked you to do the job, Walter, but you were in Egypt."

Walter Henkel grinned his appreciation of this compliment. He also was a clever man and a quick worker.

It was no coincidence that Peter Dunn was acquainted with Mr. Aaron Baumstein, the diamond merchant. He had been working with the City police on a case which touched several wholesale jewellers, but did not touch this gentleman at all, Peter discovered, when he interviewed him.

Mr. Baumstein was a thick-set, shabby-looking man, who wore a slightly soiled collar and a shabby tie and was worth two millions. He had his home in Maida Vale, and, to counteract his many admirable qualities, he had one weakness: he was a gambler in a modest way, and patronized a club near the Haymarket. There are such places in London—forbidden, it is true, by the police—but there are such places. He loved to sit for a couple of hours at a green board, happy in the knowledge that it was a perfectly straight game; and usually he rose a winner or a loser of a few pounds.

It was in the club that Peter met him for the second time. Scotland Yard was making one of its periodical round-ups, and the club in question was raided. Mr. Baumstein, with the naïveté of one who was acquainted with the police methods of other countries, asked that his name should be suppressed and offered a substantial bribe, which Peter very good-naturedly refused.

"It doesn't matter about your name; there are hundreds of Baumsteins in London. Have you any other address than the ones in Maida Vale and Hatton Garden?"

Mr. Baumstein gave the address of his mother; but, though he was cheerful in the confidence that he had escaped identification, there wasn't anybody in Hatton Garden or Maida Vale who did not know that Mr. A. Baumstein of St. John's Wood was Mr. A. Baumstein of Maida Vale.

Peter got to know him, and went to his office with greater interest because the little man was very proud of the fact that his was the only burglar-proof office in Hatton Garden. It had a foolproof system of burglar alarms. After Mr. Baumstein had locked his office and the front door, it was impossible to walk across a room, much less open a window, without a shrill bell announcing to the Metropolitan Constabulary that there were unauthorized visitors to No. 608 Hatton Garden.

"Some people spend their money on safes and

vaults," said Mr. Baumstein. "I'm all for alarms. There isn't a safe in the world that one of these American smashers can't open. I'm speaking from experience."

Mr. Baumstein could point with justification to the fact that three attempts had been made to enter his office and had failed. That scientific burglars should direct their attention to his premises was only natural: he carried a larger stock of big blue diamonds than almost any merchant in London. Peter saw them reposing in velvet cases in the steel safe in the front office.

"If you touch that handle, it rings; if you move that telephone, an alarm rings; if you open any window in the building, nothing can stop the bell ringing. Suppose somebody conceals themselves on the premises—that's the way it's always done—they could hardly move a dozen steps without setting off the alarm."

Peter was impressed.

3

Peter had forgotten Mr. Baumstein, and was still aching from the Central Midland robbery, when he received a note. It was delivered by hand to his house in Berkeley Square and was written on the notepaper of the Ritz-Carlton:

"DEAR SIR PETER DUNN,—*I wonder if you
would care to see me this afternoon at four o'clock
in my suite? I am rather thrilled by something I
have discovered in France which I think would
interest you.*"

It was signed "*Millicent Clarke.*"

It was not an uncommon name. He had a dim
idea that he had met a Mrs. Clarke before somewhere, but could not place her. Nor, when he
called that afternoon, did he recognize, in the
very dainty lady who received him, any acquaintance that he could remember.

She was rather pretty and voluble and important. He gathered that she was married and
that her husband was not in England.

"You'll think I am one of those busybodies
who plague the police," she smiled. "Harry told
me I should be snubbed for my pains, but it was
such fun that I thought I'd write to you. Just
wait one moment."

She went out of the room and came back with
a paper in her hand.

"First of all, tell me if you know anything
about that."

Peter had no sooner glanced at it than he knew
what it was: it was a bearer bond, one of a small

denomination that had formed part of the loot that had been taken from the Central Midland.

"How did you get this?" he asked.

"It *is* part of the robbery, isn't it?" she asked eagerly. "I read about it when I was in Monte Carlo, but I didn't suspect anything till I saw the little rubber stamp on the back. It is very faint—you can just see it. They evidently tried to get it out—Harry says with some kind of acid. It's true—this *is* part of the loot—is that the word?"

Peter nodded.

She was so obviously delighted by the confirmation of her suspicions that Peter found himself smiling in sympathy. He could afford to smile; out of the blue had come, from the most unexpected quarter, the one and only clue to the hiding place of the lost bonds.

"Isn't it too exciting! Harry—my husband is Harry Auburn Clarke—has been very sarcastic about me, telling me I should be a detective. But it was the rubber-stamp mark and the fact that somebody had tried to rub it away—I used a magnifying glass to find that—that made me think of the bank robbery——"

"Will you tell me how you came into possession of this bond?"

Peter should have known better than to attempt to anticipate Mrs. Clarke's story. First of all she had to tell him what her husband had said and what she had replied; then she had to explain how on three separate occasions previous to this her husband had been emphatic on a point and she had been emphatically in opposition, and it had been proved that she was right.

Peter Dunn was human and was a good audience for any pretty woman. She came back from her digressions long before he began to feel any violent symptoms of impatience.

"I met her at Monte Carlo—the woman who gave me this—Mme Kelsko or Kelski, or some such name. She was beautifully dressed, rather pretty, and very charming. She speaks English with a strong American accent. Isn't that wonderfully observant in me?"

It was at that moment that Ann Kelski became a real entity to Peter. Canvassing all the Continental crooks he knew or had heard about, he had dwelt for a moment on this lady's name, had even gone to the Record Department to search for her history, but without result.

"It was at a bridge party," Mrs. Clarke went on. "I'm afraid the stakes were high, and Mrs. Kelsko, or whatever her name was, lost. I don't like taking IOU's from strangers, and they were such terribly bad players, and I was rather relieved when she asked me if I'd take a bearer bond for a hundred pounds and give her the change, which was about twenty-five. That night at dinner I met some of the people who were at the bridge party, but nobody seemed to know who she was or how she came to be invited to the house. It was Princess Chimez Diliski's, and she does invite the oddest people. Then one day I went down to Marseilles to meet the boat which was bringing Harry back to France from India, and to my amazement I saw her. She was very poorly dressed and was walking quickly with a man. I was taking a short cut to the docks, and to my surprise they turned into one of those miserable-looking houses you find near the waterfront in Marseilles. There was no number on the door, but I should recognize it."

"Did you see her again?"

She shook her head.

"No." She hesitated, and then, with a burst of frankness: "If you think there is anything in it, I can show you the house. I'm going back to Monte Carlo the day after to-morrow to join my husband, and we could stop off at Marseilles.

He'll send the car to meet us. I know the street—
the Rue Mediterranean."

To say that Peter was elated is to put the case
mildly. He was also intensely curious. He went
back to Scotland Yard walking on air, and told
his story to the daily conference which was sitting. The chief examined the bond; a bank official
was hastily summoned, and he was emphatic
that this was part of the proceeds of the Central
Midland robbery.

Peter telephoned Mrs. Clarke from Scotland
Yard and arranged to meet her at Victoria two
days later. He spent the next day collecting such
papers as might be necessary to secure the arrest
of Ann Kelski, and, if she were British, her extradition.

4

That night occurred what Scotland Yard still
regards as the classic crime of the century. At
half-past six a policeman was patrolling Hatton
Garden. At that early hour the streets were
thronged with people, the road occupied with
vehicles, for Hatton Garden is a short cut between High Holborn and Gray's Inn Road.
The policeman was nearly opposite the premises
occupied by Mr. Baumstein when he heard the

deafening note of the burglar alarm. It was fixed outside the building two stories up, and enclosed in a perforated iron case so that it could not possibly be tampered with.

The policeman blew his whistle, and almost immediately the window on the second floor was thrown open and the figure of a frightened girl appeared.

"Is there anything wrong?" shouted the policeman, and in hysterical tones she told her story.

She was Mr. Baumstein's secretary. He had gone home a quarter of an hour before, when she was putting on her hat in the retiring room, and he had locked the door, under the impression that she had already left.

By this time other policemen had arrived, including the divisional inspector. A big crowd had gathered, not unamused by the girl's predicament. The police, realizing that what had happened was one of those minor tragedies of office life, contented themselves with dispersing the crowd, while one of their number went to the nearest telephone to call up Mr. Baumstein, who was not at home.

It was suggested that the fire brigade should be called and that the girl should be brought down, but to this she would not agree, pretending she was too frightened.

For an hour and ten minutes she stood at the window, talking to the police officer below. In the meantime Scotland Yard had been communicated with, and, knowing Baumstein's passion for cards, Peter tried a list of clubs at which the diamond merchant might be found, and in one of these he was discovered, and told what had happened.

"Secretary?" he said, astonished. "My secretary's a man, and he left an hour before I did. I have two typists, but they went out with my secretary to the post office. As a matter of fact, they asked to be allowed to go early; they were going to a theatre."

Peter jumped into a cab and went flying to Hatton Garden. Long before he reached there, the girl had left the window. The alarm bell still continued its infernal tintinnabulation; it could not be stilled until Baumstein arrived with the secret pass key which turned off the current.

He opened the door for the waiting officers, who had heard by telephone the result of his communication, and they followed him upstairs. The front room was littered with housebreaking tools; the door of the big safe hung open, a big

hole burnt in its face. There was neither girl nor
burglars to be found. A packet of sixty-three
large diamonds, valued at eighty-four thousand
pounds, and two other packets of less value had
vanished.

Peter was back at Scotland Yard when the
detailed news came through. It was a divisional
job, and, though reported to police headquarters,
no help was asked.

"The cleverest job within my recollection,"
said the chief admiringly. "The girl, of course,
appeared in the window to explain why the
alarm bell was ringing, and just as soon as she
appeared the breakers got to work, and were
working all the time she was talking to that
butt-headed copper on the street. The bell didn't
tell you what particular part of the house was
being interfered with, and naturally nobody took
the trouble to inspect the back of the premises
when it was discovered that a poor little office
girl had been accidentally locked in."

5

Peter could afford to be amused as he read the
account while going down to Dover. He explained to the vivacious Mrs. Clarke the particulars of the case; she was at first shocked, then as

lost in admiration as the most impartial superintendent.

Just before the train reached Dover she collected her belongings, and they were many:
small parcels and big parcels, handbags, rugs,
jewel case, and three books, tied together with
string, to read on the train, and a packet of
chocolates from a leading London confectioner's,
which, with her rug, she handed to Peter, towards
whom she had assumed the air and manner of a
proprietor.

At Dover a shock awaited them: a cordon of
police barred all egress; every passenger for the
Continent was informed that the French government had demanded a careful search of all baggage for contraband. Peter knew that the French
government had asked nothing of the sort, and
just what the contraband was for which they
were searching.

Mrs. Clarke was indignant, but submitted at
Peter's suggestion. He stood watching while
packet after packet was opened and examined.
It was rather a perfunctory search—for Peter
had explained to the inspector in charge that
he was accompanying this pretty lady on duty.

He saw her through the Customs on the other
side, and they entered a carriage which had been

reserved for them. It seemed to him all the time that Mrs. Clarke did not stop talking about the Baumstein robbery, which had evidently caught hold of her imagination.

"I'm sure it was a woman's idea. But, then, you don't think a great deal of women, do you? Perhaps you'll be wiser one of these days."

Just that and no more. Peter sat for a long time, thinking intently. And then suddenly she said:

"You must give me my chocolates. Harry loves the English make."

She leaned over and playfully tugged at the packet, which closely filled his pocket.

"You must let me take care of them: you'll probably lose them, Mrs. Clarke," he said.

To him the matter was plain sailing, but he was taking no chances, and, making an excuse, he went forward to the refreshment car. There were not many people on the train, and most of these were just awaking from their sleep, for they had been warned that Paris was within fifteen minutes. As Peter came back to the door of his compartment, which he had left open, he found it closed, and the blinds had been drawn down over the windows and over the glass top of the door. It was empty. As he stood looking he received a violent punch between the shoulders and staggered forward.

Peter's first impression was that it was the act of a clumsy passenger, but as he turned the door closed with a crash, and the two men who had followed him into the compartment were standing with their backs to the door, and in the hand of one was a very business-like automatic.

Peter could not see their faces. Dusk had fallen; the only light was the overhead lamp, and about each man's chin and nose a silk handkerchief had been tied.

"I'll take that box of chocolates, if you don't mind, mister; and in case you think we're rehearsing a crook play, I'm telling you that I'll plug you if you give me any trouble—I owe you one for Leary. Stick 'em up."

Peter obeyed. One of the men stepped forward and jerked the packet from his pocket.

"Sit down—and all I've said before goes." said the first speaker.

To offer resistance was to invite sudden death. Peter had an instinct for real danger, and knew exactly what would happen if he dropped his hand to the gun in his hip pocket.

In three minutes he was tied, wrists and

ankles; a big woollen scarf was wrapped round
his mouth, and he was rolled onto the floor and
under the seat. He heard the door open; two slim
ankles came into view, and presently he saw the
mocking smile of Mrs. Clarke.

"I want you to be very nice to women in the
future, Sergeant Dunn," she said. "I suppose
you guessed what was in the chocolate box—the
Baumstein diamonds—and I suppose you will
also guess I was the typist who was locked in
the office."

She was down on her knees now for greater
comfort, one slim, ringed hand resting on the
carpet. It was an hour of triumph which she
could not resist.

"I was making sure of getting the stuff away,
so I thought I'd bring a police officer along with
me to carry it! Was it clever?"

Peter could not speak, but nodded.

"That's charming of you." Her laugh was long
and silvery. He felt that in that moment she
almost forgave him his indiscretion.

A little later the train came to a standstill;
hoarse cries of "*Facteur*" came to his ears, and,
rolling out with some difficulty, he kicked at the
door. It took him a quarter of an hour to get to
the office of the station police, for he had some

business to do in the dining car, and he was not concerned at the moment about Ann Kelski.

That night Peter interviewed the chief of the police, who was not very sanguine.

"You might find her in Paris, but it is extremely unlikely," he said. "I have just had a telephone message from Le Bourget that several private aëroplanes left immediately after the train arrived. Until we check their destinations we can do nothing. More likely she has gone by car."

One of the chief's guesses was right. Ann Kelski and her two companions had been picked up by a fast car and driven back on their tracks towards the Belgian frontier. At Lille an aëroplane carried them to Cologne, where Ann Kelski had a flat.

It was a tired but triumphant woman who closed the door upon her two companions.

"I'd give a lot of money to see that poor bull's face," she said, "and a lot more to hear just what Scotland Yard will have to say to him."

She took from her bag the flat package, cut the string, and removed the brown wrapping. And then she stared: she had packed the diamonds in a red box, and this one was white.

With trembling hands she pulled open the lid —under a cover of paper shavings were chocolates. Just chocolates and nothing more, and on the top a little note scrawled in pencil:

"I have an idea you might get the diamonds away from me before I can put you in the hands of the police. In case you do, I have made certain changes. With the compliments of Sergeant Sir Peter Dunn, C. I. D."

6

"I never even guessed I was carrying the diamonds for the lady until she gave me a hint that I was not as clever as I thought I was," said Peter to his chief. "I examined the box in the refreshment car, found, as I suspected, that it contained the diamonds, and substituted a box of chocolates. The *chef de service* was very obliging: he got me one the exact size. I left the diamonds in his safe. I expected that all her boy friends would be waiting for her at the Gare du Nord, and I took no chances. Naturally, I should have pinched her as soon as we reached Paris if I could have found a French police officer. I didn't think that her gang would be travelling on the train."

"That's the one thing you should have expected," said Superintendent Leigh severely.

CASE VI

BURIED TREASURE

CASE VI

BURIED TREASURE

THERE is water in the great Sahara Desert, and
there is honour among thieves. Peter Dunn had
never struck one of these remarkable oases, but
he had been told about them by men to whom
they were rare phenomena, not likely to be forgotten.

There are certainly clean thieves and thieves
that are not so clean, and into this latter category
comes Roony Riall. When Sergeant Peter Dunn
thought of Roony, he thought of snakes.

Roony was suave, sleek, had glossy, pomaded
hair and whitish, manicured hands. He had
forged a little, taken minor parts in great crimes,
always keeping on the safety line. As a craftsman
he was versatile.

Peter loathed sly men who can never look
at you straightly. Therefore he loathed Roony,
who smiled too readily and was glib-tongued.
Nevertheless, being a police officer, Sergeant
Dunn was compelled to have dealings with him.

Peter drew the line at visits to his house, and

when Roony called one night after dinner to
impart certain information, Peter told him just
what was on his mind.

"We are always glad to meet a squealer at
Scotland Yard," he said, "but I don't want you
here, Riall. I like to keep this place clean, and
you are my idea of dirt. As a police officer I
appreciate your information, but as an individual
I tell you you have had a narrow escape from
being kicked into Berkeley Square. Is that
clear?"

Roony showed his white teeth in a smile. You
might have thought he was being complimented.

"Perfectly," he said. "I am afraid you are
prejudiced, Sir Peter. I try in my own humble
way——"

"Don't say 'humble,'" snarled Peter. "It
makes me sick!"

He jotted down the particulars the man
brought to him, but still Roony lingered.

"Have you ever thought what a marvellous
cop Dappy Lyon would be?" Roony ended the
question with a wide grin. I suppose that ten
thousand pounds reward still holds good?" he
asked.

He referred to the reward which the Trust and
Security Company had offered.

"You had better write and ask," said Peter shortly, and then: "Have you worked with him?"

"Never had the luck," Roony said.

"He is rather particular, isn't he?" said Peter offensively.

Roony smiled at the insult and chuckled to himself all the way through the hall, and was still chuckling when his unwilling host slammed the door behind him.

Peter had been engaged in relief duty when the Trust and Security Company's premises in Pall Mall were scientifically burgled. One of four men could have performed the operation, always excluding the possibility that it was the work of the Continental crowd. Scotland Yard settled down to locate the four suspects, and of these Dappy Lyon was the most important.

Exactly why he was called Dappy nobody knew. Possibly it was the work of a descriptive reporter who had a trick of covering men and things with picturesque labels. Likely enough it was a fight promoter who called him "Dapper Dick Lyon" in the period when Dappy was a featherweight, fighting for microscopic purses.

Dapper he invariably was; invariably well dressed, a generous little man who gave no trouble to the police, would go a long distance out of his way to help a fallen friend (he once paid for the defense of a man who had done him as bad a turn as any man could). He had so many admirable qualities that it was remarkable that he should have followed the career he had chosen.

If any man deserved to be called the master criminal—a title which invariably raises loud guffaws at Scotland Yard—it was Dappy. This foxy-faced little man, with a bulging forehead and not unpleasant Cockney accent, was near to being The Complete and Perfect Criminal.

He had never been convicted, though he had been several times in the hands of the police. The historical details to be found in the Record Department at the Yard contained certain interesting information. He had served in the war, had risen to the rank of corporal in the Corps of Royal Engineers, mining section. After his discharge he had worked for three years in the factory of a locksmith and safe-maker—Grindles, who supplied the strong-room doors for most of the banks. He was an exemplary workman, skilful, painstaking, ingenious. He never lost time; was popular both with workmen and employers. During the period he was so employed Grindles were making the doors for the Midland and Southern Deposit vault. It is an undoubted fact that Dappy assisted in their erection. After they had been fixed he left the plant.

Within two months of his retirement the Midland and Southern vault was opened and emptied. The exact amount that was lost nobody knows; it was considerably over a hundred thousand pounds.

Dappy was pulled in when it was discovered that he had been working at Grindles. He had (it was believed) been concerned in a previous bank robbery. He was questioned closely and released for lack of evidence. "Released for lack of evidence" became a formula in his dossier.

It was undoubtedly Dappy who organized the mail-train robbery between Southampton and London, when fifty thousand pounds' worth of bar gold was taken from the bullion van and dropped onto the permanent way through a hole cut in the floor, after the train had been slowed by a manipulation of the signals on the loneliest stretch of the line. It had not only been slowed, but stopped, and the thief had time to drop down between the lines and make his escape before the manipulated signal fell and allowed the train to proceed on its way.

He chose his men well, probably imported a few of them, paid them munificently, and made no error until he fell in love. Then his mistake almost proved his undoing. This happened about three weeks after Peter's interview with Mr. Roony Riall.

2

Dappy hadn't much use for women, never used them in any of his *coups*. He would as readily have fallen for the fat woman in a circus as for Canadian Lil, but, unhappily for him, he did not know Canadian Lil even by name. Her reputation was local to the town of Buffalo, though she had operated as far west as Cincinnati and Chicago. Roony Riall had met her in Detroit during a fleeting visit he paid there. She came to England in response to his urgent cablegram, sweetened by a bank draft that paid expenses, and he met her at Southampton, where the boat docked.

"There's fifty thousand dollars in this," he told her, "and we cut two ways."

Decoy was no new rôle to Lil. It was the main

staple of her business. She was very lovely, golden-haired, fair-skinned, modest of manner. She had planned to go to London, and had already booked her room at a fashionable hotel.

"You can get that idea out of your nut," said Roony. "You'll stay at——" He gave her the name of a less pretentious hotel in a Midland city which Dappy frequented for reasons best known to himself.

So it happened that one day, travelling to London, Dappy found himself in a first-class compartment with the lovely Miss Mortimer from Philadelphia. She was doing Europe in a quiet, inexpensive way. Her father had a small store, and she intended staying at a small hotel off the Strand. She told him all this and a great deal more.

Dappy was a kindly soul. It was a pleasure for him to help any woman. He was human, and the pleasure was intensified by the fact that she was sweet and very lovely.

Within a month they were engaged to be married. A honeymoon trip to Como was planned, and a villa was secretly rented by Dappy, who was anxious to impress her with his wealth.

In justice to Lil it must be said that she had no idea that Dappy was a very rich man. She regarded disloyalty to money as one of the cardinal sins of her profession. To her, Dappy was a crook living on the edge of comfort—that and no more.

As for Dappy, he was almost a reformed character; Miss Mortimer was the centre of a new universe. Even when they met Roony by accident in the Strand, he was not suspicious of her real character. Later . . .

"It is a curious thing," said Roony. "I recognized that little lady the moment I saw her. Her father has a store——"

Dappy knew Roony slightly. Roony's reputation was not good, but, being in love, Dappy warmed towards a man who was so full of praise for his fiancée. Out of friendliness grew confidence. Roony was given a job and the offer of a generous reward.

On a certain night the wheel of Roony's car came off in the Acton Road. The accident occurred where two policemen met at the end of their beats.

This was the occasion of the classic robbery of the Acton Branch of the Leamington and London Bank. On that night the vaults of the

bank held a large sum of money, due to liquidate
the pay rolls of several big factories in the neighbourhood. At four o'clock in the morning a
policeman tried the door of the bank, found it
open, went in, and discovered the night watchman tied hand and foot in a soundproof telephone booth.

He might have discovered this at an earlier
hour, but the motorcar accident so carefully
arranged had detained him.

The watchman could give very little information as to how he came to be in this position.
He was uninjured (this was characteristic of
Dappy's method), except that his arm bore the
marks of several punctures where the hypodermic needle had been used on him. He only
remembered a cloth being drawn over his head
and his being pulled to the ground. Beyond that
his memory was vague.

3

Dappy was in London, entrenched behind his
inevitable alibi, and considerably strengthened
by a new police regulation, introduced through
some Parliamentary busybodies, which prevented certain questions being asked of a suspect. There was no evidence on which he could

be detained, but at night he was never left unshadowed.

Roony came to Scotland Yard after a long telephone parley; in effect, he arrived under the white flag of the informer, and, although his information was sketchy and there were gaps in the story he had to tell, the chief believed him.

One evening Peter followed Dappy into a Soho restaurant and sat at his table. The little man looked up and stared at him.

"Got a gun, Dappy?"

"I never as much as owned one," he said. "Why?"

"You're coming for a little walk with me," said Peter; "and I'd like to carry your baggage."

Dappy's face twitched.

"You've made a mistake, haven't you?"

Peter shook his head.

"It's a cop," he said. "I think we've got you right this time. If you are wise, you will stand your trial for the Trust and Security Company affair as well."

A police car was awaiting them when they went out, and ten minutes later Dappy sat with four detectives.

He had been betrayed, he knew that. Somebody had squealed on him, and the situation was a desperate one. He never suspected Roony till the motorcar accident was mentioned, and then he did not suspect—he knew.

"Roony Riall, eh? Well, you've got to prove it, gentlemen, and I don't think you can. The only thing I'd like to ask you"—he addressed Peter—"is that my young lady should know nothing about this."

Peter smiled and shook his head.

"What your young lady doesn't know about this isn't worth knowing," he said. "She is a friend of Riall's—a little more than a friend, I should imagine."

They told him the truth brutally, thinking it would break him. He heard for the first time the true history of Canadian Lil. Peter saw his face go white.

Nobody knew better than the men who questioned him that, even with the evidence of the squealer, Dappy could not be convicted unless he convicted himself, but he was steadfast in his refusal to hand himself over to his enemies.

"It is pretty certain that the stuff is buried somewhere," said the chief. "Dappy is a born mole—he got a Distinguished Conduct Medal in the War for his mining work; he knows more about blasting than most miners, and you'll probably find that somewhere in England is a real Ali Baba's cave."

But if there was, Dappy was blandly ignorant of its existence. More likely, if a search had been made of the coastwise barges that went down London river by night and put into Ostend with loads of English brick, the police might have touched lucky; but nobody knew till years after that Dappy had three barges and a wharf of his own, and then the information came a little too late to be of much use.

Nevertheless, it was true, as the chief said, that he was a great digger and was an expert in the use of high explosives.

They searched his lodging without result. Every railway parcels office came under examination. Peter, who was in control of one of these search parties, never expected to find the evidence he sought. No man organized the disposal of his stuff so efficiently as Dappy.

Peter sent for Roony Riall, who came to his office. Roony was less confident.

"I tell you I was in it, Sergeant. I wouldn't own that unless it was true, would I? He worked four-handed, had two men down from Birmingham, and there was a seafaring fellow who drove the big car. I only saw him and Dappy. No, I

don't know the names of the others. After the
bust he went straight to his hotel. You found
his car? Well, maybe the stuff is under the seat."

He looked a little anxious, Peter thought, and
then his uneasiness was expressed in words.

"Does he know I've squealed?"

Peter nodded, and to his surprise Roony was
not distressed.

"Does he know about Lil?"

There was something in his voice which arrested Peter's attention.

"Why?" he asked.

"She'd get it out of him in a couple of days,"
said Roony eagerly. "He's mad about her!"

It was then that Peter realized that he and his
fellow questioners had probably committed a
bad blunder when they had played Lil.

"She's in this squeak with me," Roony went
on eagerly. "We split the reward."

"It looks as though there will be a whole lot to
split," said Peter sardonically.

There was nothing to do but release Dappy
Lyon. He could have been charged on suspicion
and a remand granted, but if, at the end of the
remand period, the police could offer no further
evidence, there would be a discharge, and the
failure of Scotland Yard would be emphasized.

Dappy was released from detention. It was remarkable that he did not employ a lawyer, and contributed nothing but his inhibitions to his salvation.

On the night he was freed Peter saw him in the West End, and, to his amazement, Lil was with him. She walked a little way from them when Peter stopped him.

"I am not believing that story about Miss Mortimer," said Dappy. "She has been bringing food to me ever since I have been inside—she's a woman in a thousand."

Peter sighed wearily.

"It must be easy to be a master criminal, with brains like yours!" he said.

Dappy spent a week in or about London, and the girl seemed to be with him every minute. They used to go for long motorcar drives together into the country—and a flying squad car, in some disguise or other, was never far behind.

One morning Dappy surprised them. He came out driving a newer and a faster car, outdistanced his shadows, heading northward. He was seen passing through Woodford. An hour later the officers were holding a consultation in the town of Epping when he appeared. Where he had been in the meantime nobody knew.

They searched his car but found nothing. That same week he left England for the Continent, and Miss Mortimer went with him.

As a matter of precaution Roony Riall had been kept under observation until Dappy disappeared. For there were odd stories told about this mild little man—Dappy was a killer, some people insisted, though Scotland Yard could never connect him with anything as romantic as murder.

Peter, being what he was, had no use for men who saw in crime of any sort the least hint of romance. He was trained in the traditions of the Yard, and the Yard, in the eyes of its staff, is not a place where unusual things happen.

If you asked the oldest inhabitant what were the most remarkable happenings within his memory, he would (after long thought) cite the inspector who cut his finger with a piece of glass and fainted, or the day the Commissioner's dog bit the clerk in the Records Department, or possibly the occasion when half the staff went sick through eating bad fish.

But of murderers who had sat in poky little rooms and told the stories of their villainies, of confessions signed with trembling hands, of great robbers who had detailed their *coups* to the chief, he would remember nothing.

4

Peter went to Berlin to supply certain information about the brothers Poliski, and his visit had nothing whatever to do with Dappy and his misdeeds. In the red building on Alexanderplatz he exchanged reminiscences with men of his own profession, and told them how badly the central heating was run in London, while they in turn remarked upon the amazing stinginess of the government in the matter of stationery.

Peter was in Berlin for seven days, spending most of his time in the Criminal Museum. One day he was walking up Unter den Linden, ruminating upon the system of traffic control, when, coming towards him, he saw Dappy Lyon. Dappy wore an elegant fur coat, though the weather was warm, lemon-coloured gloves, and patent shoes, and swung a gold-headed cane. He paused to look into a jeweller's window, and when Peter passed him he was humming "Ich liebe dich" sentimentally.

"Hello, Dap!"

Dappy looked round—he was only mildly interested in the presence of the detective.

"Doing Germany?"

"I am just having a look round." Dappy waved his hand airily to embrace all Germany. "I have never been in this country before."

"Museums and what-nots," suggested Peter politely. "You should have a look at Police Headquarters—very interesting. There are a number of scientific burglars' tools which may be new to you."

Dappy smiled indulgently.

"No more of that for me, Mr.—Sir Peter——"

"Call me Sergeant," suggested Peter. "Let us be democratic in this republican land."

"I have given up what I would describe as my career of crime," said Dappy. "I am getting married soon to one of the best girls in the world, and I'm going in for a motorcar agency. In fact, I am here in Berlin seeing my representative, a fellow named Harry Brown."

"A good old German name that. One of the Browns of Brandenburg? Or is he a Von Brown of Silesia?"

Dappy was amused.

"He's got an office on Leipzigerstrasse—telephones, clurks, everything." And then, as he saw the lift of the detective's eyebrows, he went on quickly: "He's not in Berlin just now—

doing a bit of travelling—or I'd interduce you."

"The loss is mine. Where are you staying?"

Dappy named a hotel in Kurfürstendamm, where hotels are both good and expensive. He was quite at his ease, by no means perturbed at the outrageous appearance of one who, he had every right to expect, was hundreds of miles away. It struck Peter that he was neither uncomfortable nor alarmed. He was an innocent man, conscious of his temporary virtues.

Peter went back to the Adlon in a speculative mood.

"The office" did not allow Adlon accommodation, but Peter never stinted himself in the matter of comfort. His first act was to put through a call to Dappy's hotel. He found, as he had expected, that the little man had spoken the truth. He was staying at the hotel and occupied a suite which could not have cost him less than a fiver a day. And Miss Mortimer was living at the same hotel.

Peter saw them driving in the Tiergarten in the cool of the evening, and he himself did not escape observation.

"That's Dunn, isn't it?" asked the girl.

Dappy nodded. He was toying with her hand absently.

"The man who said I was—a bad woman? Where did he get that nerve?"

"Just trying to rattle me, my love," said Dappy. "He isn't a bad fellow——"

She was not disposed to discusss so uninteresting a matter as Peter Dunn, and came back to the subject that his appearance had interrupted.

"I never did believe you were a burglar, Dicky," she said. "And even if you were, why shouldn't you be? Pa always says that property isn't distributed like it should be. I wouldn't mind if you were a crook—really! But I know, of course, that you are not. How could you have got rid of all that jake—money, I mean—Pa always calls it jake—without the police knowing? You would have to be a mighty clever burglar to do that!"

The bait of crude flattery had been cast in front of him before. This time he bit.

"Oh, wouldn't I? You don't know me! Listen, kid." He turned to her with sudden energy. "I don't know what this fellow Dunn is doing in Berlin. Maybe he has got something on me." He paused and frowned. "If I thought so I'd tell you something." He patted her hand. "I don't want my little girl to be left without money. I've got twelve thousand pounds—that's sixty thousand dollars—cached near London, and in case anything happens to me I am going to tell you just where it is. Sixty thousand dollars of real money!"

She was breathing quickly. He was easier than she thought.

"You'd find it, because I have got the whole thing laid out."

He lowered his voice, although there was nobody to hear him except the taxicab driver, who certainly spoke German and probably spoke Russian. "Remember how you and me went sweethearting to that wood—Epping Forest?"

She nodded.

"Remember my carving the letters of our names on that big tree?"

She nodded again. She could find the place blindfold. It was a little off and close to a side road, and the tree stood in the centre of a grassy clearing; the names had been cut largely, if awkwardly, and between them an odd-looking triangle which was designed for a heart.

"It is at the foot of that tree. You couldn't miss it." And then, unexpectedly: "Are you fond of Roony?"

She was fonder than she would admit, for Mr. Roony Riall had been very attentive since she came to England. They, too, had planned a little trip together.

"Where did you get that idea?" she said scornfully. "I have got one boy in this whole wide world, and that's my Dicky."

Dappy sighed—she hoped happily.

He had some work to do and left her in the sitting room, telling her he would be out for at least two hours.

He was hardly out of the hotel before "Miss Mortimer" went to the telephone and put through a London call. It was half-past ten in the evening, which is half-past nine in London, and the line was clear; she was through to Roony in ten minutes.

"Got it?" said his anxious voice. "My God, you never have! Did he tell you about the Trust and Security——"

"Trust nothing!" she answered brusquely. "Get a paper and put this down. Sixty thousand for the lifting! You know the main road to Epping through that wood?"

Her instructions were very explicit and not to be mistaken. Roony Riall wrote feverishly and read back to her the instructions she had given.

At that moment Dappy was in Peter Dunn's sitting room at the Adlon. There was a whisky-

and-soda on the table before him, and he was
being confidential.

"I am leaving her, Sergeant; in fact, my baggage is at the station. I don't think that Miss
Mortimer and me will get on together. No, I'm
playing fair—I never left a woman flat in my
life. I have paid the hotel bill and stuck five
thousand marks under her pillow. A bachelor I
live and die, Sergeant. Women can be useful,
but not in my line of business."

"When are you going?" asked Peter.

"To tell you the truth—to-night," replied
Dappy. He smiled faintly. "Clever fellow,
Roony Riall, cleverer than me!"

5

At eleven o'clock that night an Essex policeman saw a car turn from the main Epping road
and stop a little distance down a side road. He
watched the car for some time, but it was too
dark to see the man who alighted and, with the
aid of a hand lamp, made a search for a certain
tree. Later the policeman saw the flash of the
lamp and was walking towards it when he saw a
flash of white flame and felt the shock of a terrific
explosion that almost blew him off his feet.

When he recovered balance and wits, he ran in the direction of the sound.

There was a big hole at the foot of the tree. The force of the explosion had stripped away the bark, and with it certain initials carved sentimentally. Three policemen searched all night to find fragments of an unknown man who had exploded the mine which an ex-Corporal of Engineers had so skilfully buried.

CASE VII

THE PRINCIPLES OF JO LOLESS

CASE VII

LONG before Peter Dunn had succeeded to the baronetcy, when he was plain Detective Dunn, he met Henry Drewford Lesster, though he never retained a very vivid impression of that unfortunate young man. It was on a night when he met other graduates of the great university—to be exact, on Boat Race night—and Mr. Lesster was one of half a dozen boisterous and hilarious young gentlemen whom he had been called upon to eject from a West End theatre.

Mr. Lesster had appeared before a police magistrate and had paid his fine. The only thing that Peter ever remembered about him was that he spelt his name with two s's. It was just this odd circumstance of memory, that he should remain as an identity among thousands of other arrests and detentions.

Two years later the accident occurred on the Worthing Road. A big touring car, driving towards London late one Sunday night in June,

157

crashed into a small car, in which a London doctor was driving his wife and two friends back to town. One of the men passengers was badly injured. The big car had its radiator and bonnet smashed, the small machine was a wreck.

Fortunately, there was near the spot a cyclist-policeman, who was practically an eyewitness of the accident, if such events can be witnessed in the dead of the night. He came up, rendered first aid, and sent the injured man in a passing car to a hospital before he carried out the routine of taking numbers, examining licenses, and jotting down particulars of the accident.

The big car was undoubtedly on the wrong side of the road. The driver, a dazed young man, smelt strongly of drink. His license bore the name of Henry Drewford Lesster.

The constable was young and inexperienced, or he would have known that it was his duty to take the driver to the police station and to charge him with a very serious offense—that of being drunk while in charge of a motorcar—or, at any rate, to submit him to the tests which a police surgeon would impose. Instead, he took particulars from the license, warned the delinquent that he would be summoned, and allowed him to proceed on his way.

There was no question—the man was drunk. The driver of the small car was emphatic on that point, and when in the night the injured man died, the unhappy constable was suspended by his inspector for his failure to make the arrest.

Scotland Yard was communicated with, and it fell to Peter Dunn to make inquiries about the motorist—one of those odd jobs that make up the life of a sergeant of the C. I. D.

The address was an expensive flat in Park Lane, but he found it in the possession of a wealthy stockbroker who had taken it for two years.

"Mr. Lesster has been ill for some time and he is living in the country with an aunt."

He had the address, which Peter copied into his book—Deeplands, Kensham, Berks.

Deeplands was an old Queen Anne house that lay in the middle of about six acres of unkept ground. There was a general air of neglect about the place. The windows, except two or three that lit the drawing room, were shuttered and dirty. There was about it an atmosphere of mystery which appealed even to one who professed to despise mysteries as creations of imaginative writers.

Peter knocked and pulled the big, iron-handled bell. It was a long time before he heard the bars being removed and a key turned. A tall, broad-shouldered young man, with a red, unshaven face and hair that had not been brushed or combed, opened the door. Peter thought he was a caretaker until he heard him speak, and then he realized that it was the voice of an educated man.

"Well, what do you want?" he asked suspiciously.

When Peter stated his business he shook his head.

"Mr. Lesster is not staying here; he is abroad. He went abroad six months ago."

"Is this his house?" asked Peter.

The man hesitated, and as he did so a voice spoke from the hall behind him. He opened the door a little wider, and a middle-aged woman came sweeping across the parquet floor. "Sweeping" literally—she wore a dress which had almost a train. Her hair was "brassily" golden. Her face, an old-looking face, was powdered and rouged. On one arm was a mass of diamond bracelets.

"You want to see my nephew?" she asked harshly. "He went to the Continent this morn-

ing. He came home last night with his car
smashed up, and took his smaller car and left
very early. He said he was going to Paris."

Peter was puzzled. He recognized a relationship between the sot who had opened the door
and the grotesque woman, and learned soon
after that they were mother and son.

"This gentleman told me he had been away
for months——" he began.

"My son knows nothing about it," she said
harshly. "He went to bed early last night, and
he didn't know that Henry had returned. He
only comes here occasionally. Would you like
to see the car?"

How would she have known that he had come
to make inquiries about the accident? This
woman was a shrewd guesser, he thought, and
became suddenly interested in her. It was not
an unusual type, the woman who refused to
grow old and clung to the illusion that art could
revive the past glories of youth.

Picking up the train of her dress, she led the
way to a big garage, and he saw the damaged
car and made one or two notes in his book.

"You are a police officer, aren't you? I expected somebody would call. Henry is very wild.

He is consumptive, you know, and he started drinking about a year ago. He is a great worry to me."

"Where do you think I shall find him?"

She shook her head.

"I haven't the slightest idea. He disappears for months at a time and never takes me into his confidence."

"Who are his lawyers?" asked Peter.

Again she shook her head.

"I don't think he has any. I hold his power of attorney, but I have never had to use it."

2

The cabman who drove Peter back to the station gave him one or two interesting items of news about Deeplands.

"We have had some queer fish living there," he said. "One was a German who called himself, Schmidt. I am the only man who knows what his real name was—Egolstein. Is there such a name?"

"Egolstein?"

Peter was immediately interested. Was it a coincidence?

"He is the fellow that got twenty years for robbing a mail boat—I saw his picture in an old paper. That's how I knew it was him," said the cabman.

Then it *was* Egolstein, the most dramatic and sensational bank smasher of his age.

Peter asked a question.

"Oh, no, he was no relation of Mrs. Lewing or Mr. Lesster—Mr. Lesster took the house after Egolstein went away. It belongs to a parson."

The driver had never seen young Mr. Lesster, though he knew he used to stay at Deeplands when he was ill.

"Funny thing, there has been another man after the house," said the loquacious driver (his conveyance was an open touring car, and Peter sat by his side). "There was a young gentleman down here only last week who tried to look over it, but Mrs. Lewing and young Mr. Lewing were out——"

"And the servants would not admit them?" said Peter.

"There are no servants. The old lady and her son do all the work in the house. Rum lot, ain't they?"

Peter agreed that they were a rum lot; but then, the world was full of rum lots, and he took no further interest in Deeplands until Jo Loless called upon him.

Peter Dunn did not like old lags. He stead-
fastly refused to believe in their penitence, and
when they told him that they were going straight
and that all they needed was a couple of pounds
to buy a new kit of tools so that they could start
work next Monday morning, it was his practice
to say things which would have sounded cruel
and harsh to the sentimentalist who did not know
the peculiar psychology of the professional
wrongdoer.

There had been a time when he had taken the
trouble to look up the records and to discover
exactly the trade for which the mythical kit of
tools was intended, but now he turned down the
ill-written pleas automatically.

Naturally, there was a certain variation in the
begging letters which came to him. Sometimes it
was requested that he should advance eighteen
and twopence for the purpose of taking the
writer to his dying father, brother, aunt, sister,
or wife, who lived in a town just that distance
from London. Occasionally the appeal was a
pathetic request that he should make a small
loan to get an overcoat out of pawn.

It may seem curious to all except those who
understand the queerly intimate relationship
between the police and the criminal that such

requests should be made at all; but those who are acquainted with the inner working of Scotland Yard know how frequently they come to every officer, and especially to an officer reputedly as rich as Sergeant Sir Peter Dunn.

The request of Jo Loless might have shared the fate of its fellows but for its unusual character. Jo wanted nothing less than a letter of recommendation, not to the landlord of a house which he was desirous of renting, but to its present tenant. It was apparently a fairly large house; he wrote of it vaguely as being "in the suburbs of London," and the rent was two hundred a year, which is an unusually high one for a house in such a situation, and amazingly expensive for a man in Jo's position.

Peter was on the point of throwing it into the wastepaper basket when something peculiar in the phraseology caught his eyes, and he read it again:

"During the time I was in Dartmoor (as you know, Sir Peter, I have been just released), I worked out a formula for making malleable glass. I put a little money by and have enough to furnish the place and pay the rent for two years, besides keeping myself. The house I have decided upon is

ideal for my purpose. I think the present tenants could be persuaded to let me have the house if they knew you were interested in me. Frankly, my outrageous request is that you should help me by giving me a letter to them telling them, not that you are a friend of mine, but that you are interested in my acquiring the house."

Peter read the letter and frowned. It sounded like a lie, and yet Jo Loless would not lie. He was a shrewd confidence man, a glib teller of stories, who had gone down for five years for a brilliant job which had miscarried owing to the activities and intelligence of the man to whom he was writing.

Jo Loless had had a good education and was a clever business man. Peter read the letter for the third time and, taking a sheet of paper from his stationery rack, scribbled an invitation for Jo to call.

He liked this suave, rather good-looking rogue, who had graduated from one of the medical schools into a more or less strenuous method of gaining a livelihood, who never ceased to jest about his appropriate name and its psychological influence in the determination of his career, and never adopted any other. He was, indeed, one of the few crooks whose names appeared in the annals of Scotland Yard who had never adopted an alias.

3

Jo called after dinner the next night, a debonair figure in correct evening dress, and not even the most suspicious of mortals, seeing his fashionably cut clothes, would have imagined he had a few months before been working behind the walls of Dartmoor prison. His hands were perfectly manicured, his hair glossy and well brushed. He wore pearls in his white shirt-front, and the thin cigarette case he took from his white waistcoat pocket bore a monogram in diamonds.

"Sit down, Jo, and help yourself to a drink," said Peter. "Had a bad time?"

Jo pulled up the knees of his trousers very carefully and exposed his silk-covered ankles, then sat down.

"I do not drink—you've forgotten my habits," he said. "No, it wasn't so bad as you could have wished."

"What's the idea of this house? What is it called, by the way?"

"Deeplands," said Jo, and Peter stared at him. "May I?"

Jo took out a cigarette and poised it inquiringly. Peter nodded, and he lit it.

"I like the place; it's got about six acres. The
house is in a shocking condition, and a couple of
ghastly specimens are living there, but I will
have the place put right. It is away from the
beaten track. Incidentally, it is just outside the
Metropolitan Police area."

"Malleable glass!" Peter's eyebrows rose.

"Why not?" said the other coolly. "It is one
of the dreams of scientists, more practicable
than the philosopher's stone, but only just.
There is, I believe, a big, old kitchen in the house
that would make a marvellous laboratory—I
was in the laboratory at Gresham, if you will
examine my dossier, and I was rather keen on
chemical research work. I have cached enough of
my illicit gains to keep me comfortably for
a year or two, and I might have a very amusing
time, without troubling you fellows, with a
possibility that in the end I can build up a big
fortune."

Peter was watching him keenly.

"Do you think you will succeed?"

Jo pursed his lips.

"I don't know. The trouble with me, Dunn, is

that I have principles. Before now I have sacrificed a considerable fortune rather than stray from what to me are the permissible paths of wrongdoing. Possibly I shall lose another."

"But why that house?" asked Peter. "And why should a letter from me influence the tenants you are trying to dispossess?"

Jo shrugged his shapeless shoulders.

"I don't know."

He looked at Peter for a long time.

"You have never done time in Dartmoor, of course—it's a pity: it is a humanizing experience. There was a man there—a German—one of the biggest smashers of his time—Egolstein."

Peter nodded.

"You knew, of course, that he lived at Deeplands? I was in the village yesterday, and the gentleman who hires cars to the unsuspecting stranger informed me that he had told you. Egolstein and I worked in the same shop. He loved Deeplands; he wove about it a certain glamour which it probably does not deserve. To me it became synonymous with quiet and calm and restfulness. I admit I was shocked when I saw the place, but the illusion of its peacefulness appealed——"

"Marvellous," murmured Peter.

"You think that I am pulling one, but I am not."

Jo was earnest, or appeared earnest.

"Poor old Egolstein, who died, as you know, in the prison hospital, gave me a dream to realize. It was terrible to find the house in the possession of a wicked old lady who drinks and her son who soaks. The first time I saw them she wanted to let the place; the second time she would not open the door to me, and the letter I sent her was answered with a rudeness which was unbecoming in one who has passed the meridian of life."

He stopped and looked at Peter.

"How can a letter from me help you?" Peter asked. "Is there any special potency in my name?"

Jo shrugged again.

"I have an idea there is," he said.

What was behind this?

Peter's mind was working quickly. He was receiving no very satisfactory reactions.

"Who is the landlord?"

Jo took a card from his pocket and laid it on the table.

"That's the address—The Reverend William Walkier. He is a rural dean and rolling in money.

Deeplands estate had seen a flash of light near the house. He was a local man and knew that both Mrs. Lewing and her son had left that morning for Brighton. He rode his horse through a gap in the hedge and galloped up to the mansion. As he did so, he saw the figure of a man slip into a plantation near the back of the house and shouted to him. From the fact that the man broke into a run it was evident that he had no business there.

The policeman made no attempt to pursue this suspicious-looking intruder, but, continuing to the house, he dismounted and made a brief survey. By the light of his pocket lamp he discovered that a pane of glass had been broken, a window sash raised, and the shutters forced. Thinking there might be a caretaker in the house, he rang the bell, but, receiving no reply, had ridden back and telephoned his report to the nearest police station.

4

At this period there had been a number of country-house robberies, and Scotland Yard had been called in. Peter Dunn drove down to Deeplands, and, joining a local inspector, came to the house the same way as the robber.

There was a considerable amount of silver in the untidy dining room, and this had not been disturbed. One of the back doors had been unlocked and opened, they discovered—it was near this that the light had been seen.

Their search of the house revealed nothing, except a number of rooms which were shut and locked, a considerable state of disorder and uncleanliness, an immense number of empty wine bottles, but nothing which gave the slightest clue to the intruder's identity except that on one of the tables there was a small basket which contained the remains of a meal.

In such a big and rambling house the search could only be brief and unsatisfactory. Peter was inclined to accept the theory of the local inspector that the thief "had been disturbed."

Attempts to get into communication with Mrs. Lewing and her son failed—he learned this the next day by telephone.

There was another and more important work for Peter—a big fur robbery in the East End of London.

When he returned home that night, the butler, who admitted him, told him that there was a man waiting to see him.

"The gentleman who came a couple of months ago, sir—Mr. Loless."

Peter frowned.

"Loless? What does he want?"

He had almost forgotten the existence of the confidence man.

Jo was sitting in a deep armchair, thoroughly at home. He wore a lounge suit, and by the side of his chair was a small attaché case, to which he waved his hand with a smile as Peter entered.

"Foresight!" he said.

"What do you want?" asked Peter.

Mr. Loless smiled again.

"I require an interpretation of the law," he said. "You will observe that I have come prepared for immediate arrest. Do you know the old Latin tag about a cobbler sticking to his last? I have departed from that excellent advice and have tried burglary."

Peter looked at him with astonishment.

"Are you surrendering?"

Jo nodded his head gracefully.

"In a sense," he said. "Of course, the story of the malleable glass was a lie. It deceived most people, but it did not deceive you. I certainly wanted to scare her ladyship from her domain, because I was pretty sure she had something to be scared about. She and her son were drunk for a week after you paid them a visit. Can I have a drink?"

Peter rang the bell, and no word was spoken until the servant had left the visitor with a whisky-and-soda.

"I have been drinking steadily since yesterday morning," said Jo, sipping the amber liquor. "It is not as amusing as I thought it would be, but it does take away unpleasant memories."

"Well?" Peter was curious.

"I was orderly in the hospital at Dartmoor," said Jo, "and attended Egolstein in his last moments. He told me that he had buried thirty thousand pounds' worth of currency in the cellar of his house, Deeplands. Very naturally, I was anxious to secure that money, but in the meantime a new tenant had moved in and was difficult to shift. When they went off to Brighton—they are staying at Thirty-four, Lieland Crescent, by the way—I broke into the house."

"You were the burglar?"

Again Jo inclined his head.

"There is a cellar, and underneath that another cellar. You will find the door behind a large packing case, and beneath *that* cellar Egolstein had buried his money. I dug down to it. I hate manual labour: it makes one hot and blisters one's hands; but thirty thousand pounds! It didn't want a great deal of digging, because somebody had already loosened the earth. I noticed the bricks had been replaced. When I searched——"

The hand that lit his cigarette trembled a little.

"Odd that they should have chosen the same place, eh? That poor young devil must have died or been murdered a year ago, but they kept it quiet. You will be able to determine the exact cause of death. As an embryonic medico, I should say he had been shot. The old lady held his power of attorney and a lot of blank cheques. The son used his motorcar and his license. He had lost his own, you will find, through drunkenness."

Jo sighed heavily as he threw his just-lighted cigarette into the fireplace.

"If I had been a heartless brute I could have gone on digging and got the money, but I have my principles, Dunn. It is a nice point of law: do I get five years for burglary, or a large reward for discovering a couple of cold-blooded murderers?"

CASE VIII

THE DEATH WATCH

CASE VIII

THE DEATH WATCH

LEE SMITT had no police record and no apparent nationality, though he claimed to be American, and the claim was not disputed. Certainly he had lived in the United States, and it was pretty easy to locate the area, for in the early days he had the rapid-fire lingo of the Middle West, which is so disconcerting to the leisurely Southerners and a source of amusement in New York.

Red Fanderson was undoubtedly American, and had probably come from English stock who were Sanderson in the days when people wrote S's like F's.

Joe Kelly was just cosmopolitan: he knew Paris, spoke French rather well, had seen the inside of two French prisons, and had had a narrow escape of taking the rap at Cayenne, which is frequently and inaccurately referred to as Devil's Island, for Devil's Island is only a bit of it.

They came unobtrusively into London in the

days when Sergeant Peter Dunn was newly come
to the Criminal Investigation Department and
was sitting at the feet of Inspector Sam Allerway,
learning his business.

There were quite a number of people who
thought that when he succeeded to his title and
fortune, he should have retired gracefully from
the force.

A certain lordly relative once expressed this
point of view, and Peter asked:

"When you became Lord Whatever-your-
name-is, did you give up golf?"

"No," said the staggered aristocrat.

"Very well then," said Peter.

"I really don't see the connection," said his
baffled lordship. "Police work isn't a game?"

"You don't know the half of it," said Peter.

And here he was, learning his business from
Sam Allerway.

There was nobody more competent to teach a
young officer than Sam. He was a great detective,
the greatest in our generation. He might have
reached the highest rank, but he drank a little,
gambled a lot, and was notoriously in debt, and
therefore suspect; though Sam had never taken
a cent from any illicit source in his life.

There is a popular delusion that high officers at

Scotland Yard own rows of houses and have considerable investments. No doubt very large presents have been made and accepted by grateful citizens who have benefited by the genius and prescience of men at Scotland Yard. It is against all regulations, but it is not against human nature.

Perhaps, if Sam had been offered some big presents by the law-abiding people he had helped, he might have accepted them, but all his offers had come from the wrong end of the business.

"You can't learn this too soon, Peter," he said. "The crook's money has got two hooks to it—and those hooks never come out! This doesn't affect you, because you've got all the money in the world, and I know just what's going to happen to the bird who tries to slip you a monkey for giving him five minutes to get out of the house."

Sam Allerway was never a popular man with his superiors. His acid gibings made him no friends. He had a trick of summarizing the character and the disposition of his chiefs in one biting and uncomplimentary phrase, and, but for the fact that he was a brilliant thief-catcher, he would never have progressed as far as inspector.

One of the few people who respected him and understood him was a certain J. G. Reeder, who at that time was associated with the Bankers' Trust as their private detective and investigator; but as Mr. Reeder does not come into this story it will be sufficient to sum up the character of Sam Allerway in his words:

"The criminal classes would be well advised," he said, "and be giving no more than what is due, if they erected a statue to the man who— um—introduced old brandy into our country."

Old brandy was Sam Allerway's weakness. But he was perfectly sober on the night the Canadian Bank of Commerce was robbed of 830,000 Canadian dollars.

The robbery was effected between five o'clock on a Saturday afternoon and seven o'clock on the Sunday morning. Three men had concealed themselves in an office immediately above the bank premises. The Canadian Bank of Commerce was situated in a large corner block facing Trafalgar Square.

The lower floor and the basement were entirely occupied by the bankers, the five floors above being given over to various businesses, that immediately above the bank premises being occupied by an insurance company. The block had been specially built and was the bank's property. Between the insurance office and the banking department was a concrete floor which was further strengthened by an iron grid set in the centre of the solid concrete.

On the day of the robbery Trafalgar Square was filled with an organized demonstration of the unemployed. Parties arrived from various parts of London, each headed by a band and carrying their banners and slogans. All the police reserves were gathered to deal with possible disturbances.

Another favourable circumstance for the burglars was that a section of the roadway before the bank was being torn up to deal with a faulty gas main. All that afternoon with the indifferent music of the brass bands there had mingled the staccato rattle of automatic roadbreakers.

There could be no question that pneumatic drills were also used by the burglars, and that they synchronized their operations with those of the workmen outside. The concrete dwelling was broken through immediately above the manager's office, which was locked, and to which the two watchmen on the premises had no access.

As to whether there were two watchmen present or not when the floor was pierced is a question which has never been satisfactorily settled. Both men swore they were on the premises, but it is almost certain that one of them went out for an hour, and during that hour the thieves got into the manager's room, unlocked the door on the inside, slugged the one remaining watchman, whom they surprised as he was looking through the plate-glass window at the demonstrators, and tied him up.

The second watchman was knocked out near the side entrance of the bank, in circumstances which suggested that he must have come in from the outside at some time in the afternoon, since there was no hiding place where his attackers could wait except behind the door.

The two men were blindfolded before they were tied up and gagged. They were unable to give any description of the burglars, and, but for the circumstance that the first man had been blindfolded with one of the robber's own handkerchiefs, which bore a laundry mark, no evidence at all might have been secured that would convict them or even give the police a reasonable clue.

The three men had an excellent kit of tools. They were able to open the vault door, cut through the bars of an inner grille, and remove every scrap of currency in the vault.

Every hour the bank was closed a patrolling policeman, passing the side entrance of the bank, pressed a small bell push and waited till he received an answering clang from a bell set in the wall. Evidently the thieves knew the bank method thoroughly, for he and his relief received all the signals until eight o'clock. At that hour, when the policeman pressed the bell, he received no answer. He tried again, but with no further success, and in accordance with practice he reported the fact to headquarters at Cannon Row, which is Scotland Yard.

He then made his way to the front of the bank and peered in. Two lights were burning, as usual, and there was no sign that anything was wrong. He rapped on the front door, received no answer, and waited here until a squad car came from headquarters, carrying his immediate chief, and, what was more important, duplicate keys of the bank, which were kept at Cannon Row in a case, the glass of which had to be smashed before they could be taken out.

The discovery of the robbery was immediately made. One of the two watchmen was sent off to hospital in an ambulance, the second taken to the station for questioning. Within half an hour the big chiefs of Scotland Yard were at the bank, making their investigations, and Allerway was allocated to the case.

"This is not an English job," he said, when he had made an inspection of the tools. "It is a Yankee crowd or a French crowd, and it's nine to one in favour of America."

"I suppose," said his chief, who did not like him (he was afterwards dismissed for incompetence by the Kenley Commission), "you're going on the fact that the tools are American made? Well——"

"They're English made," said Allerway, "as you would have seen if the Lord had given you good eyesight and you weren't too lazy to look."

Allerway used to talk like this to chief inspectors, and that was why he was not particularly popular.

He began his search like the workman he was. By the Monday morning he had identified Red Fanderson as the owner of the handkerchief. He had a room off the Waterloo Bridge Road, and a search of this led Allerway to a very high-class hotel in the West End and to the discovery of a gentlemanly guest who had left on the previous day after ostentatiously labelling his baggage for Canada.

Here Allerway had a lucky break. There had been staying in the hotel a southern European royalty, who had been photographed by a news-paper man as he left the hotel one morning. Quite unconsciously Mr. Lee Smitt, who had also chosen that moment to leave the hotel, had appeared in the background. With him had vanished his valet, Joseph Kelly, pleasantly spoken, a favourite in the couriers' room, and quite a modest personality.

The police throughout the country were warned. A week later Sam picked up a new clue. A man answering Lee Smitt's description had purchased a second-hand car and had it regis-tered in the name of Gray. He had chosen an American car of a very popular make.

"The number plate——" began the garage man.

"You can forget the number plate: he's got another one by now," said Sam.

It was Peter Dunn's first big case, and he was thrilled. He hardly got any sleep in the first week of the chase, and on the night the three men were located he was ready to drop; but the news that the car had been seen passing through Slough galvanized him to life.

It was a foul night; rain was pouring in buckets, and a gale of wind was sweeping up from the southwest. They picked up the trail at Maidenhead, lost it again at Reading, cut back to Henley without any greater success. At six o'clock in the morning the car was seen at Andover and a barrage laid down, but Lee doubled back towards Guildford. It was on the Guildford Road that they came head to head, the squad car and that which carried the wanted men. Lee tried to dart past, but the squad driver rammed him.

There were in the police car, besides the driver, only Peter Dunn and Inspector Sam Allerway, but the three men offered no resistance.

Peter took charge of the prisoners, and Sam drove the car back. They stopped at a little wayside inn, and here Sam searched the car. He found nothing in the shape of property. There were two suitcases, containing the belongings of the prisoners, but no money.

It was curious, the number of people who had seen Lee Smitt and his three companions, if not leaving the bank carrying a suitcase, at least in the vicinity of the bank. Yet they might have escaped conviction on the ground of insufficient evidence if Sam Allerway had not dug up from a railway luggage room a duplicate set of bank-smashing tools. It was on this evidence that the three men went down for twelve years.

It was this evidence which spurred Lee Smitt to make his remarkable statement, that in the car when he was captured were four packages of Canadian currency value, $60,000. Smitt told the judge that Sam had promised to make it light for him if he could slip these in his pocket and forget them. It was a crude lie. Peter Dunn stood in the court raging. But it was one of those lies which had possibilities. People read the account and said: "Well, I wonder . . . ?" There was a departmental inquiry. Sam Allerway was crushed, beaten. He turned up for the meeting of the board, drunk and truculent, and was dismissed the force.

A fortnight later they picked his body out of the Thames.

Two years after that Peter Dunn was the principal witness at another staff inquiry, and the chief inspector who had been responsible for Allerway's ruin was dismissed with ignominy and narrowly escaped a term of imprisonment.

Where was the bulk of the money taken from

the Canadian Bank of Commerce? Scotland
Yard thought it had been sent abroad, divided
into thousands of small sums and sent through
the post to an American address. It was a simple
method of disposing of paper currency, and practically undetectable.

Interrogated at intervals at Dartmoor, Lee
Smitt hinted that this had been the method of
disposal. But there were shrewd men at Scotland
Yard who pointed out that at the time the money
had been stolen the men had been fugitives, and
that there had been a special watch placed by the
post office on all bulky packages addressed to the
United States.

Peter's own report on the case is worth
quoting:

"These three men arrived in England six
months before the robbery, which was not only
perfectly planned, but their getaway was as
skilfully arranged. They had a car to take them
to the coast, but this was damaged in a collision;
otherwise the second car would not have been
purchased. Lee Smitt is a man with an American
police record: he was concerned in three bank
robberies, was sentenced to from five to twenty
years in Sing Sing, but was released on a techni-
cality when the case went to the Appellate Court.

He is a man of brilliant education, and there is no evidence that he had any confederate in the United States. Every important bank in America has complied with the request of Scotland Yard to render an account of suspicious deposits made by mail from England, and nothing out of the ordinary has been discovered."

Nine years later the three men were released from Dartmoor, escorted to Southampton, and put on a boat bound for the United States. The New York police reported their arrival. And that, so far as Peter Dunn was concerned, was the end of the case.

2

It was in the late summer of the next year that he became acquainted with the Death Watch, and in the strangest and most unusual circumstances.

Peter Dunn was taking a vacation. His idea of a vacation was to hire a little cabin cruiser and move leisurely from Kingston to Oxford, camping at night by any promising meadow, stopping at the towns to purchase his supplies and, with the aid of a gramophone and a small library of books which he brought with him, pass the evenings that separated him from the morning's plunge in the river and another day of progress through a procession of locks towards the historic city he knew so well.

Between Lockton and Bourne End the hills rise steeply. It is a wild and a not particularly cheerful spot in the daytime. He arrived at his anchorage late at night, tied up to the weedy bank, pulled down the fly-proof shutters of his cabin, and cooked his evening meal.

It was not a night which attracted holiday makers to the river. A drizzle of rain was falling; a chill wind blew down the river, and when the sun set he was glad to pull on an extra warm pullover. He did not know this part of the river at all, and had a feeling that it was some distance from a road. He neither saw motorcar lights nor heard the hum of engines.

Peter cursed the English summer, pulled close the door of his little cabin, and spent ten minutes destroying such inquisitive flying things as had found their way into the interior.

He was trying to read a German work on criminal practice, but found it difficult to keep his eyes open. At nine o'clock he got into his pajamas, extinguished the little reading lamp, and slipped into bed.

He was not a heavy sleeper, but certain notes

woke him more quickly than others. He could
sleep through the heavy rumble of traffic and
the sound of deep-throated klaxon horns, but a
shrill note amidst the noise would wake him
instantly.

He was awake before he realized he had been
asleep. It was a woman's scream; there was no
doubt about it. He heard it repeated and tumbled
out of his bunk, listening. It was a scream of
terror—somebody was in horrible fear.

He pulled a waterproof coat over his pajamas,
pushed open the door of the cabin, and came out
to the little well deck. Somebody was crashing
through the undergrowth. He heard a woman's
sobs.

"Who's there?" he called.

Going into the cabin, he found his hand torch
and sent a powerful beam into the darkness.

The girl who was found by the light stood,
terrified, staring towards him. She was in her
nightdress and an old, discoloured robe. Her hair
was awry. The round, moon-like face was dis-
torted with fear.

"It's all right," said Peter.

Evidently something in his voice reassured
her, for she came scrambling down the steep
bank.

"Don't come any farther. I'll pull my boat in. What is the matter?"

She did not answer until he had grabbed the mooring rope and drawn the stern of the boat into the bank. The hand he took was deadly cold, and she was shivering from head to foot.

"Get me away out of here—get me away quickly!" she sobbed. "That horrible thing . . . ! I wouldn't stay another night. . . . I heard the death watch, too, and I told Mr. Hannay, and he only laughed."

"You've seen something disagreeable, have you?" said Peter.

He had taken her to his cabin and put a rug around her. An unprepossessing young woman, he classified her without difficulty, and when she told him later that she was a housemaid he was rather surprised that she had attained even to that position.

He had some hot coffee in a thermos flask, which he had put away against his early morning breakfast. He gave her this, and she became more coherent.

"I work in Mr. Hannay's house, sir . . . it used to be one of Diggin's Follies. You know the place?"

"No, I don't know the place," said Peter. "Who is Mr. Hannay?"

She was very vague about Mr. Hannay, except that he was a rich gentleman "in the drapery."

Apparently it was the death watch that worried her. She had heard it again and again. Two other servants had left because, when the death watch sounded, something always happened. She had heard the click-click-click of it in the wall.

"When you hear that, somebody's going to die."

"I know the superstition," said Peter with a smile. "It's a little beetle, and he's quite harmless."

She shook her head.

"Not here, sir." She was very serious. "When you hear the death watch at Chesterford something always happens."

Peter heard a voice hailing the boat from the bank and went outside. He saw a tall, thin man who carried a torch in his hand.

"Have you seen a girl?" asked a booming voice.

"I've got her here—yes," said Dick.

"I'm Mr. Hannay, of Chesterford." The voice

had a certain pomposity and self-importance. "One of those stupid servants has been making a fuss because she heard the death watch and thought she saw something . . . she ran out of the house before I could stop her."

"If you please, sir"—the girl had come out of the cabin and stood behind Peter—"I was so frightened, sir."

"Come back to the house immediately," said Hannay's voice. "Really, it is too absurd of you, making me ridiculous and making yourself ridiculous. Ghosts! Whoever heard of ghosts?"

"I saw it, sir."

"Rubbish!" said Mr. Hannay. "Come along. I'll take you back to the house."

Peter was a little relieved. He had no particular desire to accommodate a young lady for the remainder of the night. His little clock told him it was just after midnight, and he did not relish the prospect of sitting up all night with a companion whose only topic of conversation was ghosts and death watches. He helped the girl to the shore.

"Thank you very much, Mr.—uh——?"

Peter did not oblige him with his name. He was glad when the girl had gone, but for an hour he lay, turning from side to side in his bunk, speculating upon this strange little adventure. Death watch? Ghosts? He smiled.

He was just dozing off when there came another interruption. He got out of bed and again went out of the cabin, not in too good a temper. The man on the bank had no lantern.

"Excuse me, sir, are you the gentleman that gave shelter to Lile?"

For a reason best known to himself Peter went suddenly cold.

"Yes," he said quietly.

"She took away your rug. Mr. Hannay asked me to return it to you."

All Peter's irritation was gone now. Dimly he could see the man on the bank. He had left his lantern in the cabin, but evidently the man on the bank could see him.

"Will you catch, sir?"

Something was thrown at him; the soft mass of the rug struck him in the chest.

"Have you got it? Good-night, sir."

The man went scrambling up the steep path to the invisible house. Peter stood for a long time, the rain pattering on the shoulders of his waterproof.

"Good Lord!" he said softly.

He went back to the cabin, switched on the light, and sat down.

"Who the dickens was Diggin?" he asked aloud at the end of an hour of thought. "And what was his peculiar brand of folly?"

He left his moorings just after daybreak, stopped at Marlow, and went ashore, and at that unearthly hour engaged a room at the Red Lion, where he finished his interrupted sleep. At ten o'clock his boat was still moored at the big boathouse, and Peter was pursuing inquiries.

Diggin was a builder, long since dead. He had conceived the idea of building two villas on the crests of two identical hills. They were not good villas, but they were very precious in the sight of Mr. Diggin, who had been both the architect and the builder. They suffered from this disadvantage, that they were near no main road, were indeed almost unapproachable, since in the days when they were built the motorcar was an unknown method of transport. They were red brick villas, with bow windows and slate roofs, altogether unlovely, and they were called "Diggin's Follies" because nobody wanted to buy them or hire them. Even the advent of the motorcar did not make them any more desirable.

The week before his death Mr. Diggin had sold one and the land on which it stood to a man who intended starting a poultry farm. He had never started it. The second, and more important, sale was conducted by Mr. Diggin's executor, and the purchaser was Mr. Hannay, who had so built onto this villa that it had lost its native ugliness and had attained the dignity of a country home.

"In fact, Chesterford is one of the nicest houses in these parts," said Peter's informant. "It has beautiful grounds, a bathing pool, and everything."

Mr. Hannay apparently was a wholesale draper who had passed his responsibilities on to a limited liability company in the days when company promoters were paying enormous sums for likely propositions. He had one child, a daughter—her name was Patricia. Peter had a glimpse of her, driving a big Rolls through the town. She wore a blue tennis jacket, and a gaily coloured scarf about her throat. Her head was bare, and her brown hair was flying in all directions. Pretty, he thought; but then, Peter had this weakness, that he believed most women were pretty.

His very discreet inquiries produced no stories

of ghosts—at least, no ghosts attached to Chesterford. Yet something peculiar was happening
in Mr. Hannay's house. Servants were leaving;
few stayed there more than a week—this he
learned at a local employment agency. The butler
had left a month before and had been replaced.
Two cooks had left in one week; there had been
five new maids in the house in the past two
months.

Mr. Hannay was a gentleman of irreproach-
able character. He was rich, a churchgoer, had a
large electric canoe and two cars. Obviously he
was not a flighty man: a plain, matter-of-fact,
sober, rather intolerant citizen, so far as Peter
could make out. There had been some feeling
locally because, at a recent Parliamentary elec-
tion, he had discharged two gardeners who had
had the temerity to vote for the Labour candi-
date and, very foolishly, had boasted of their fell
deed.

He was, in fact, the kind of man one might
meet in any small English town, who believed
that the country was going to the devil and that
something ought to be done about it.

Three days of his vacation Peter gave up to
a little private investigation. He went near
enough to the house to catch a glimpse of Miss

Patricia driving the yellow Rolls, and was considerably impressed.

The household, he discovered, consisted of Mr. Hannay and his daughter, a working butler named Higgins, two maids, one of whom had left in a hurry—Peter supposed this was his terrified guest—and a gardener-chauffeur who had recently been engaged.

Peter made a very careful survey of the grounds, but did not approach the house. It was easier to examine the second of Mr. Diggin's Follies, for the red brick villa stood more or less as it had been delivered from its maker's hands: an atrocity of a building, gaunt, desolate. It stood in two acres of untidy ground. No attempt had been made to form a garden; the weeds were knee-high; the windows blurred with the rains and dust of years. In one part of the field—it was little more—he found the old chicken huts that had been delivered years before and had been stacked at the back of the house. The weather had taken toll of them: most of them had fallen to pieces.

He cleaned a pane of glass with his handkerchief and stared into an empty room, the walls of which had been covered with a paper of atrocious pattern. It was peeling from the walls, and as he stared he saw a little brown form whisk across the floor and disappear into a cavity which he identified as the fire grate.

"Rats and rubbish," said Peter.

He tried the doors, front and back: they were locked. At the back door he thought he saw the trace of a footprint, but this was not remarkable: the people in the neighbourhood often came over to stare at Diggin's Folly; they overran the surrounding ground, and would have picnicked there if its bleak character had encouraged such a frivolity.

About twenty years before, the gloomy house had gained notoriety as the scene of a very commonplace murder. A tramp woman had been murdered by another wanderer of the road, who had long since fallen through the trap in expiation of his crime. It was when he was making inquiries about this deserted place that Peter heard the first hint of a ghost.

The place was reputedly haunted, or had enjoyed that reputation till the public grew tired of its mystery. Yet Peter discovered an elderly man who had seen the old tramp woman walking in the grounds of the house, wringing her hands and moaning.

"I admit I'd been drinking that night," said

his informant, "but I know when I've had enough."

"That," said Peter, "is a more common illusion than ghosts."

He had three weeks' vacation. Nearly a week of it was gone. He went up to Scotland Yard and saw his chief.

"Surely, you can have six weeks if you want it. It's due to you, but you told me that three would be sufficient?"

Peter explained that he needed the rest. He had just finished with an important and tiring case, and the extra leave was granted.

He had another object in coming to town. He collected his car. Peter Dunn was a rich man. It was the complaint of Scotland Yard that he ought not to be there at all.

He came back this time to Maidenhead. He did not want to be at Marlow too long, and with his car the question of distance was no object.

It was not to be supposed that his presence in the immediate neighbourhood of Chesterford should pass unnoticed. After dinner one night Pat Hannay asked a question.

"A young man? Good heavens, I don't notice young men! One of the maids' admirers—that new girl, Joyce, is rather pretty."

"He doesn't look like a maid's admirer," said Pat. "In fact, I cherish the romantic impression that he might be waiting to catch a glimpse of me."

"Nonsense!" said her father.

"You're very rude," said Pat, and then: "Do you realize that we know hardly anybody in this neighbourhood? We've got a lovely tennis court that nobody plays tennis on, and even my London friends do not come to Chesterford."

Mr. Hannay looked at her in amazement.

"Why on earth do you want people here?" he said. "Half the delight of the country is that one is alone."

"It isn't half my delight, or even a quarter of it," said Patricia Hannay, and went on without a pause: "He was rather nice looking."

"Who was?" asked her baffled father. "Oh, the young man you saw? Well"—heavily jocose—"why don't you ask him to play tennis with you?"

"I thought of that," said Pat, and then struck a more serious note. "You know the cook has left?"

"Has she?" said Mr. Hannay in astonishment. "I thought to-night's dinner was extraordinarily good——"

"I cooked it," said Pat. "It was rather fun, but if I did it more than twice it would be a bore. Daddy, do you realize what an awfully ugly house this is?"

She was touching Mr. Hannay's tenderest point. He was an amateur architect. It was his boast that he had designed the additions that had turned a villa that was plain to the point of ugliness into something which bore a resemblance to a charming country house.

"I don't mean that the architecture's ugly," said Pat, hastily tactful, "but it's so isolated, and I can almost understand the servants getting ideas about ghosts and groanings and rappings. Why don't you let it, Daddy? That was a magnificent offer you had the other day."

"Let it?" scoffed Mr. Hannay. "Absurd! It would be—um—derogatory to my position. I can't let furnished houses. I either close them up or sell them. I was saying to Dr. Herzoff at the club—he's an excellent player; in fact, I had all my work cut out to beat him——"

She had heard of Dr. Herzoff before.

"Is he living at the clubhouse?"

"I don't know where he's living—at some hotel in the neighbourhood. A charming fellow, with a tremendous sense of humour——"

"Which means he laughs at your jokes and hasn't heard your ancient stories, Daddy. Does he play tennis?"

Hannay thought he might.

After tea the next night Pat strolled out down to the lower garden. Beyond the trim box hedge ran a road which had not been a road at all until Mr. Hannay had made it. It was here she had seen the mysterious young man who had excited her interest. She wondered what he would say if, with the boldness of despair, she invited him to a game of singles. She was a little disappointed that she had not the opportunity of making this test.

That night there came a crisis in the affairs of Chesterford. Pat was in that pleasant stage between sleep and wakefulness when she heard a shrill outcry. She sat up in bed, listening. From somewhere near at hand she heard a "click-click-click," and, despite her philosophy, shivered.

The death watch! She had heard it before, but not quite so distinctly. Again came the scream. She reached for her dressing gown and slipped out of bed. In another second she was in the corridor.

The maid's room was at the end of the passage. She tried the door; it was locked, but the incoherent babble of sound which came from within told her she had not made any mistake.

Mr. Hannay had heard the cry. Pat turned her head at the snap of his lock. He came out, a gaunt figure, more exasperated than frightened.

"What the devil's the matter?" he asked.

Pat did not answer. She was rattling the handle of the maid's door.

"Joyce! Joyce! What is the matter? Open the door."

The key turned and the door opened. Joyce stood there in her nightgown, her eyes staring wildly.

"Oh, miss, I saw it!" she gasped. "I saw it as plainly as . . ."

"Saw what?"

Pat brushed past her into the room, closing the door. The girl fell back on the edge of her bed, her face in her hands.

"What did you see?" asked Pat again.

For a little time the maid did not speak.

"It seemed to pass through the door, miss," she said in a hollow tone, "and I locked the door before I came to bed. It walked slowly past me and sort of disappeared . . . it was almost as if it walked through the wall."

"It was a nightmare," said Pat, her heart quaking.

Joyce shook her head vigorously.

"Oh, no, miss, it wasn't. There was no nightmare about that. It happened, just as the other girls said it happened. And I wasn't asleep; I was wide awake—as much awake as I am at this very minute."

Pat meditated for a second. She simply dared not ask any more questions: this type of terror grew on what it fed on. Then her natural curiosity overcame her discretion.

"What was it like?"

"A horrible-looking man. He had a terrible face. Dressed in tramp's clothes . . . dirty-looking . . . he was awful. There was blood on his hands; it seemed to be dripping as he walked!"

Pat looked at her helplessly, then went to the door and opened it.

"May my father come in?"

Hannay was standing outside.

"Joyce says she saw a ghost—a tramp or something, with blood on his hands."

"Stuff and nonsense!" growled Mr. Hannay. "She must have been dreaming."

The maid looked up at him resentfully.

"It's not stuff and nonsense, sir, and I've not been dreaming."

She got up suddenly from the bed, walked to the window, and, drawing aside the thick curtains, peered out. Pat saw her draw back, an expression of horror on her face.

"Look!"

Hannay pushed her out of the way, and, throwing open the casement window, thrust out his head. Then a chill ran down his spine, for he saw the man distinctly. He was tall, grotesque in the moonlight, a figure that moved and made strange and hideous noises as it walked.

"That's him," quavered Joyce. "Do you hear? That was what I heard . . . quite near, miss!"

There was perplexity on Hannay's face, anxiety on Pat's, twitching terror on the face of the maid. Pat supposed, with a quiet malice, that the girl found some enjoyment in her terror —was at least laying the foundation for horrific stories to be told to her friends.

"I was wide awake. He came so close to me I could have touched him."

She seemed loth to leave the subject.

"What did he look like?" asked Mr. Hannay.

"She's told you once," said Pat impatiently.

But Joyce was not to be denied her narrative.

"His face was horrible!" She shuddered.
"Like a man who was dead!"

"Come into the library," said Pat to her
father.

She turned to the maid.

"You'd better wake up Peterson and get him
to give you something hot to drink."

They left the girl sitting on the edge of the
bed, covering her face with her hands. Mr. Hannay led the way, walking to his desk in the library. It was the one spot in the house where he
could command any situation. And here was a
situation which asked for command. Yet, as was
his wont, he waited for a lead from his daughter.
Mr. Hannay initiated nothing. He found the
weak place in the suggestions of others, and by
this process, which operated throughout his life,
he had amassed a fortune.

"Father, we've got to do something."

Nobody knew this better than Mr. Hannay.

"Well, what do you expect me to do?" he
asked.

There was an obvious solution, and she suggested it.

"Send for the police," she said.

Her father snorted.

"And make myself a laughing stock! Police—ghosts! I've never heard such nonsense! Don't you suppose that that idea has already been considered by me and rejected?"

"What are we going to do about it?" she asked squarely. "Daddy, I can't go on; this thing is getting on my nerves."

It was getting on Mr. Hannay's nerves also.

"It is all very stupid," he said.

There was a little pause as he thought, his head on his hands.

"That man I met at the golf club . . . Professor Herzoff—he's a very well known scientist. Have you heard of him?"

Patricia shook her head.

"Neither have I," admitted Hannay naïvely. "It's very odd, we were talking about ghosts. I don't know what fool brought it up. He believes in them."

Pat stared at him.

"Is he grown up . . . and believes in ghosts?"

"He's grown up and believes in ghosts," said Hannay firmly. "I'll bring him over to-morrow morning. He might give us a new angle to the situation."

It was not the first time Mr. Hannay had

evaded the big issue. Always to-morrow something would be done. Pat sighed.

"I want a new cook to the situation," she said.
"That's the third servant we've lost in a fortnight. After all, these people *have* seen things."

"I don't believe it," said Mr. Hannay irritably. "It's all imagination. Ghosts—bah! Death
watches—rubbish!"

She held up her finger to enjoin silence. From
somewhere near at hand the death watch was
tapping rhythmically, noisily, ominously.

3

Mr. Herzoff—when he was called "Professor"
he generally protested—was a man of middle
height, spare of frame, delicately featured. His
hair was grey; his long, rather sensitive face almost colourless. Behind his horn-rimmed glasses
were a pair of dark eyes, and the stare of these
could be very disconcerting.

It was generally believed at the Mansion Golf
Club that he was wealthy. He used to speak dis-
paragingly of his little house at Weisseldorf, but
from what he said once they gathered that his
little house was a respectable-sized castle.

His appearances at the club were of a fugitive
character. He had been a member for many

years, but when he made his last appearance the staff had almost entirely changed. He played a good game of golf, was quiet, unassuming, and an authority on almost every kind of subject from economics to wild-game hunting.

Mr. Hannay found him singularly sympathetic when, a little shamefacedly and with understandable hesitation, he broached this question of the supernatural.

The Professor must come over and see his house. Mr. Hannay was very proud of Chesterford, and never tired of exhibiting it. Most people who accepted his invitation had gone away unimpressed. Mr. Herzoff, on the other hand, stood before the house and pointed out certain admirable features of architecture which its designer had never noticed before. Mr. Hannay, with some pride, personally conducted his guest through the house. They came at last to a drawing room which owed much of its loveliness, if the truth be told, to the insistence of the builder upon certain characteristics, for which Mr. Hannay now took all the credit.

"If I may express the opinion, it's a very beautiful home," said Mr. Herzoff.

Hannay agreed.

"All that panelling came out of the Duke of—

well, I forget his name, but anyway he was a duke; had a château in France. I've had big offers to let it, but no, sir! A man from London was up here a month ago, trying to get it. He told me to write my own cheque."

"I can understand your reluctance," said Herzoff politely, and waited for the story which had been promised him. "You say something happened here last night?"

Mr. Hannay took a deep breath.

"I am going to tell you," he said. "There have been some queer things happening here. At least, these servants say so. I tell 'em that the death watch is all nonsense. It's a little beetle that gets into the wood and starts knocking to attract the attention of the female beetle."

Mr. Herzoff smiled. He knew the insect.

"That is what it has all grown out of," said Hannay. "They think the tapping means some-body's going to die. That is the superstition. You get one or two hysterical girls around the place and they'll imagine anything."

Mr. Herzoff appeared thoroughly interested.

"What have they heard or what have they seen?" he asked.

Mr. Hannay explained.

"I don't believe in it—understand that. They

must have left the wireless on one night. They heard voices talking—people quarrelling. Then the old cook saw a man walking on the lawn. Some down-and-out looking around for a place to sleep, I imagine. Last night the maid saw him again."

Mr. Herzoff frowned. His dark eyes focused upon his host. Evidently he was impressed.

"They heard people quarrelling—a man and a woman? That's queer," he said. "That's very queer!"

"Why, what do you mean?" asked Hannay, alarmed.

The Professor did not attempt to explain what he meant. He asked one or two questions. What time was it at night when this quarrelling was heard? When he was told eleven, he started.

"Is there any significance in that?" asked Mr. Hannay anxiously.

"No," said the other slowly. "Only I would rather like to be here at eleven o'clock one night."

"Would you?" asked Hannay eagerly. "I was hoping you would offer to do that. I'll have your things brought over from the hotel."

Mr. Herzoff hesitated for the fraction of a second.

"You'd be doing me a favour," Hannay went

on. "I'll tell you the truth, Mr. Herzoff. All this talk about ghosts and voices is getting me—er—rather worried."

Herzoff looked at him thoughtfully.

"I don't want you to believe for one moment that I am an authority on the occult. I have dabbled in it just a little, as every scientist must. Generally speaking, all this ghost business has a very simple explanation. Either somebody is trying to fool you or somebody is lying to you. If you see it yourself, that is quite another matter, but it is not conclusive. If you think your daughter won't object to my staying——"

"She'll be delighted," said Hannay, with great heartiness.

Pat had been into Marlow, shopping, and was approaching Quarry Hill when there shot out of the Henley Road a business-like little racing car. She swerved violently to the left and jammed on her brakes, hot with annoyance, not unconscious of the fact that she herself had been travelling at a very good speed.

Peter Dunn, who drove the offending car, stopped within a few inches of her running board and eyed her reproachfully.

"There is a notice telling you to go slow," said Pat indignantly. "Can't you read?"

Peter shook his head.

"No; I can do almost everything but read," he said calmly.

She was breathless, still angry, yet mindful of the fact that here within a few feet of her sat the mysterious young man whose constant appearances near the house had excited her interest.

"You might have killed me," she said.

"I might have killed myself, which is also important."

His callousness and effrontery took her remaining breath away.

"Very charmingly put," she said, maintaining her politeness with difficulty.

"I'm very sorry to have frightened you," he said, and that was exasperating.

"I'm not frightened! Do you mind backing your car so that I can go on?"

He made no attempt to move.

"Can't you go on unless I back my car?" he asked innocently.

"Can't you see?"

She was furious with him.

He nodded.

"Well, do something, please!"

And then he asked a surprising question.

"Aren't you Miss Patricia Hannay?"

"That is my name, yes," she said coldly.

"Good Lord! What a bit of luck! You're the one person in the world I want to meet. My name is——"

"I don't want to know your name," she said haughtily.

"The first name is Peter——" he began.

"I'm thrilled," she said. "Will you please back your car?"

Peter's gesture was one of despair.

"May I make a confession? This is a new car, and I don't know how it works. I only know the self-starter and the brake."

She looked at him suspiciously.

"It doesn't sound true, does it? Well, it isn't. Before I back I want to ask you something, Miss Hannay; and, first, I want to apologize to you for giving you such a fright."

"If you imagine I'm frightened by a——" She hesitated for a word.

"Say it," he said gently. "Don't spare my feelings. 'Brute' was the word you were thinking of——"

"I wasn't," she said tartly, and looked round.

A car was behind her, waiting to pass.

"We're holding up the traffic."

But he was indifferent.

"I'll bet nothing frightens you—bad driving, collisions—ghosts——"

He paused inquiringly, and saw her start.

"What do you mean—ghosts?" she said, a little breathlessly. "What do you know?"

Peter shrugged his shoulders.

"I was in a boat the other night. One of your maids came flying down the hill, babbling of bogeys."

She did not reply, but just stared at him. And then:

"Will you let me go?" she asked.

He put his car into reverse and drew clear, and her machine jerked forward and went flying up Quarry Hill. Peter followed at a more leisurely pace, but when he came to the open road at the top she was out of sight.

So that was the man? . . . She was not quite sure of him. Usually she could place men—especially young men—but for the moment he eluded classification. He was not unpleasant, but she resented his assurance, which made her feel something of a fool, certainly a little on the inferior side.

As she came up the drive to Chesterford she saw a stranger standing by her father's side under the white portico, but she instantly recognized him by the description her father had given as the redoubtable Herzoff. Mr. Hannay introduced him.

"I'm afraid I'm taking advantage of your father's hospitality, Miss Hannay—I am the unexpected guest."

She smiled at this.

"Not altogether unexpected. We're rather glad to have you. I hope you won't die of indigestion, for the new cook will not be here for two or three days."

Apparently he had been on the point of leaving when she arrived. He was driving over to his hotel to collect his baggage. She thought that, if she had not known who he was, she would have placed him as a scientist. He was what a scientist should look like, she thought.

"It will be charming to have him, but why is he coming to stay with us just now?" she asked. "By the way, does he play tennis?"

Mr. Hannay shook his head.

"I'm afraid he doesn't. The fact is, he's rather keen to go into this ghost business."

She made a wry little face as she walked into the house.

"Does he know all about it, too?"

"Why 'too'?" asked Mr. Hannay with a frown, and she told him of her adventure.

"I don't know who this young man is, but apparently the fact that we are troubled with ghosts——"

"Don't say 'troubled with ghosts,'" said Mr. Hannay irritably. "It sounds as though we were troubled with cockroaches."

"They're worse than cockroaches," said Pat. "Well, he's heard about them . . . this young man."

"Who is he?" asked Mr. Hannay.

Patricia, peeling her gloves, sighed impatiently.

"I don't know, Daddy—he's just a young man. And rather impertinent. No, I wouldn't say that—not impertinent. But he's a little unusual."

"Does he live about here?"

She changed the subject.

"What did you tell Mr. Herzoff?"

Hannay was rather vague. He had told him about the voices and the people talking and the death watch. . . .

"Did you tell him about the dog that was found dead on the lawn?" she asked quietly.

Mr. Hannay winced. That was the one subject that he did not discuss. He had bought a dog, a trained police dog, and it had died in most peculiar circumstances. Higgins, the new butler, had been the sole witness, and there was the dog, stiff on the lawn, to support the testimony.

Higgins came in at that moment, a melancholy-looking man, with a weakness for taking away drinks that had not been drunk and tidying things unnecessarily.

"You saw it, Higgins?"

"Yes, miss, I saw it. You were talking about the dog, sir? I don't want to see anything like it again."

"He might have been poisoned," growled Hannay.

Higgins shook his head sadly.

"Why, sir, who could have poisoned him? I was watching him. He walked out onto the lawn. I could see him plainly in the moonlight. And then I saw this woman in white come out of the trees, and she sort of lifted her hand. The old dog howled and just dropped."

He took his handkerchief from his trousers pocket and dabbed his forehead with great precision.

"And the next minute, sir"—impressively—

"I heard the death watch—right in my room where there isn't any panelling."

"Why didn't I see it?" asked Hannay irritably, and Higgins looked pained.

"Because, sir, if I may respectfully suggest it, you were asleep, and therefore you wasn't looking. And if you was asleep and wasn't looking you couldn't see anything. That's been my experience, sir. It's got me, sir." He was very serious. "I've been with some of the best families in the country and I've never seen anything like this happen."

He looked round over his shoulder as though he expected to find some supernatural eavesdropper.

"The house is haunted, sir," he said in a lowered voice.

"Nothing of the sort," snapped Hannay. "I will see just what is going to happen."

Higgins sighed, gathered up the glasses onto a tray, and shook his head.

"You won't see anything unless you keep awake, sir—that's my experience," he said.

"I'll keep awake all right," said Hannay grimly. "Have a bedroom got ready for Professor Herzoff. He's coming to stay here to-night."

When Higgins had gone:

"The death watch, my dear, as I have explained before——"

Pat groaned.

"Is a little beetle ringing up his girl friend—I know all about that. I learnt it at school," she said.

She met the new gardener that afternoon. It was no unique experience to come across odd people working about the house whom she had never seen before. It was less of an experience to meet servants in the morning and find they had disappeared by the evening.

She came across a big man working with a hoe on the edge of the lawn. He grinned at her and nodded. He was not a pleasant sight. He had broad shoulders and a round, odd-looking head. His features were irregular; he had the biggest and ugliest mouth she had ever seen in a man.

"Are you the new gardener?" she asked.

He grinned again.

"Yes, miss, I am. Name of Standey. I'm a bit new to this place, so you'll have to excuse me."

She remembered then that there had been no flowers in the house for two or three days, and told him.

There was something about him she did not like. He was staring at her with frank admiration.

There was in his attitude an insolence which she resented.

"I don't see why they want flowers when you're around, miss," he said, with clumsy gallantry. "I don't think I am likely to grow anything as pretty as you."

She stared at him, open-eyed. This was a new experience for her, and not a particularly pleasant one.

"Go up to the house and see the maid," she said coldly. "Ask her what flowers she wants."

He did not stir: he stood, leaning on his hoe, his pale eyes devouring her.

"I'll be going up to get my tea in a minute——" he began.

"Go up now," she said, and he went reluctantly.

She told herself it was the sort of thing she must expect if they engaged incompetent servants. The man was probably a gardener's labourer who had seized the opportunity of promoting himself to a position which he could not adequately fill.

From the lawn to the box hedge which surrounded the western confines of the property was only a few yards. She was unaware that she had attracted an audience, and not until she heard a soft laugh did she turn round quickly. It was the young man who called himself Peter.

"What a lad!" said Peter. "One of the old cave-man school."

Recovering from her surprise, she looked at him coldly.

"He was very impertinent," she said. "There seems to be an epidemic of that sort of thing."

Peter grinned.

"And I am part of the disease?" he said. "Yet the last thing in the world I want to be is impertinent. What is his name?"

She was eyeing him steadily, and there was no encouragement in her glance.

"I didn't ask him for his card," she said, "and anyway, you can't read," she added maliciously.

Peter grinned again.

"That was a little joke. I should have explained it at the time. All my jokes require an explanatory footnote. As a matter of fact, I am a pretty good reader."

She nodded.

"There is a board on the gate you came through," she said significantly.

"I know," said Peter. "It says 'Private. Please keep out.' I thought it was unnecessarily brusque, even rude."

For some reason or other she was exasperated; unreasonably so she agreed to herself.

"You're lucky not to have met the dog——" she began.

"He would have been lucky to have met me," said Peter quietly. "I understand your dog died with dramatic suddenness after seeing a ghost."

"Who told you that?" she gasped.

"*Je sais tout*—French. As a matter of fact, I'm terribly interested in your affairs, Miss Hannay. I know it's abominable of me, but I can't know too much about you, and if I could only have a talk with you for ten minutes——"

"The odd thing is that I don't want to talk to you even for one minute."

She saw him look past her and turned her head. Standey, the new gardener, was coming away from the house and walking towards her.

"That isn't odd—it's inhuman," said Peter. "You ought to be ashamed of yourself."

"Is that all you have to say?" she asked stiffly.

"You've got a guest coming, haven't you? He dresses for dinner—one of the old Austrian aristocracy."

She half turned to leave him, but it was not so easy: the temptation was to go on talking.

"The gardener's coming back. Perhaps you'd like to ask him what he wears for dinner."

She saw Peter's face cloud.

"No, I don't think I'll wait for your attractive henchman," he said. "You and I will meet another time, perhaps."

"I hope not," she said.

She was a little startled that the fact of the gardener's presence should make him withdraw with such speed. What interest did Chesterford have for him?

Later in the afternoon she saw him again. At the western end of the property, where the ground began to slope down towards the river, was a thick belt of pine trees. Here, even before Mr. Hannay had improved the property, was a black wooden hut, which was now used to house the lawn mower and other garden implements. He was standing against this, turning over with the toe of his shoe a big heap of mould that was stored there. She hesitated for a second and then began walking towards him, but Peter saw her coming, and when she had rounded a big rhododendron bush which for the moment obliterated a view of the hut, he had disappeared.

He had been very much interested in this heap of earth and in the wheel tracks which led from the hut. He had tried to open the door, but it was fastened with a staple and a patent padlock.

He went to the car he had parked in the side road and drove off. His inquiries that morning had located the cook who had recently left. She was staying with relations on the Reading Road —a stout, placid woman, who was very disinclined to discuss her late employer. After a while, however, Peter persuaded her to talk.

She liked Mr. Hannay; she thought Patricia was "a sweet young thing"; but for Chesterford itself she had little use.

"I don't mind burglars and tramps," she said, "but it was these goings on at night that worried me. Howlings and shriekings, and people fighting on the lawn—it got so bad, sir, that I couldn't sleep."

She believed in the death watch. The demise of her own mother had been foretold. She had heard the tick-tick-tick of this mysterious agent, and a picture fell from the wall for no reason that was ascertainable.

"What other noises did you hear at night?" asked Peter.

She had heard a sort of thudding, she said vaguely, as if somebody were digging. Then one morning she had come down into her kitchen and found that the door had been forced. There were signs of muddy feet on her clean floor. Whoever it was had left a key behind.

"A key?" said Peter quickly. "What sort of a key?"

The ex-cook smiled broadly.

"Would you like to see it?"

"Have you got it?" asked Peter eagerly.

She had brought it away with her as a souvenir of her alarming experience. Going out of the room, she came back with an old-fashioned-looking key in her hand. It had rusted but had been recently cleaned.

"It didn't belong to any of our doors; we've got those patent little locks—what do you call them?—with flat keys. Yale locks. I meant to give it to Mr. Higgins, the new butler who came in, but I forgot."

"Would you mind if I kept it for a day or two?" asked Peter.

She demurred at this.

"I don't know whether I ought to do that. It might open somebody's door, and I should feel responsible."

Ultimately he persuaded her, and he went back with a clue which, he told himself, might not be a clue at all.

When he got back to his room he examined the key carefully. There was no maker's name on the handle; it was, in fact, the type of key which fitted a lock which was not made nowadays. Then an idea occurred to him, and he sat up. It would fit the kind of lock that Mr. Diggin would have chosen.

4

The Professor came over in the afternoon, and Pat was a little startled when she heard that the Professor was dressing for dinner. This was unusual: neither Pat nor her father dressed except when they were going out. She hastily changed her dress to match the splendour of their guest.

Since he had arrived Mr. Herzoff had spent his time making a minute inspection of every room in the house, including her own. He had followed this up by a very careful survey of the grounds; but he had nothing new to offer at dinner in the shape of a solution. Since Pat was very human, she was pleased with his praise of her dinner.

Mr. Herzoff was the most satisfactory guest they had had. He liked his room; he thought the view charming. His presence, at any rate, had one pleasing result: no sound disturbed the stillness of the house that night, and even the death watch maintained a complete silence.

Peter Dunn spent a long time on the telephone that morning: a longer time communing with himself. He strolled through the crowded streets of Maidenhead and stopped before a second-hand bookshop. Outside were a number of shelves on which the gems of literature of other ages were displayed. He saw one stout volume, read the title, and grinned. The title was—*Advice to a Young Lady of Fashion.* The price was two-pence. Peter put the heavy volume under his arm, not knowing exactly how his jest might develop.

It developed unusually, it turned out, for that afternoon he had a sudden spasm of panic, and in the centre of that panic aura floated the trim figure of a girl who, for some reason or other, had become very important to him.

He spent the afternoon working clumsily, and left just before sunset, with the bulky book in his pocket. He waited till dark before he approached Diggin's Folly. The gaunt house was an ugly smear against the evening sky when he drove his car into its grounds and cautiously approached the house.

Taking from his pocket the key the cook had

given him, he inserted it in the front door. His heart beat a little faster when the key turned and the door opened to his touch. The hinges did not squeak as he had expected. He had sufficient curiosity to stop, after he had shut the door, and examine them with his hand-lamp. There was oil there, recently applied.

He waited, straining his ears, but there was no sound except the scurry of tiny feet. Generations of rats had been born and lived in this deserted building. Every step he took sent some terrified rodent to cover.

He went from room to room on the ground floor and found nothing. He climbed the stairs that creaked under him, inspected three small rooms, and found them empty. The door of the fourth was locked.

From his inside pocket he took a flat leather case, fitted a pick-lock to the handle, and probed inside the keyhole. Presently the wards shot back; he turned the handle and entered.

Somebody had been living here. There was a table with three empty china jugs and a couple of plates on it. In a cupboard he found two new empty suitcases. Continuing his search, he made a startling discovery. In another cupboard, whose lock he picked, he found, wrapped in oil-paper, three automatic pistols of heavy calibre, and stacked near them six boxes of cartridges. He rewrapped the pistols, locked the cupboard, and went out of the room, carefully locking the door behind him. He did not go to his car, but pushed through the hedge which separated Hannay's property from its desolate neighbour.

The chances of seeing Pat were, he knew, remote, unless he went to the house and asked for her, and that was the one thing he did not wish to do.

As he came along the fringe of pines he thought he saw a man crossing the lawn towards the gate, and he drew back under cover. Apparently he had been seen, for the man stopped, and Peter sensed, rather than saw, that he was looking in his direction.

He could see the light in the drawing room. Evidently dinner had finished. Peter sat down on the stump of a tree and waited patiently for developments.

There was a feeling of tension at Chesterford that night. The servants felt it. Pat had a sense of foreboding which she could not analyze or understand, and when Joyce asked if she might stay up in the kitchen with Higgins she pretended she did not know why the girl should prefer the company of that uninspiring man to the comfort of her own little room.

"I suppose," said the Professor when the girl had gone, "she is still shaky over what happened last night—the man who walked through her room? By the way, was the door locked?"

Pat nodded.

"But the window was open."

"It was much too small for anybody to get out that way," said Hannay.

Higgins came in at that moment. He looked a little perturbed.

"Excuse me, sir, have you another guest coming to-night?"

Hannay shook his head.

"Why?" asked Pat quickly.

"There's a man been hanging around this house ever since dark," said Higgins. "I saw him slip back into the wood when he saw me."

"When was this?" asked Hannay.

"About five minutes ago. As a matter of fact, I thought I saw him in the garden this morning, talking to you, miss."

Pat felt her face go red and was furious.

"Somebody talking to you in the garden this morning?" said Hannay, frowning.

Pat nodded.

"Yes, it was the man I . . . his name is Peter. I told you about him."

She was a little incoherent.

"But it's absurd, Higgins. He wouldn't be here to-night. Why should he be?"

She made an excuse a little later and went to her room. Mr. Hannay looked after her.

"I've never seen Pat like that," he said slowly, but evidently the Professor was not interested in the unusual behaviour of Miss Patricia Hannay.

After the door closed on her he sat for a long time, his fingertips together, his eyes on the carpet.

"Do you mind if I speak very plainly to you, my friend?" he said.

Mr. Hannay was quite willing to accept any amount of plain speaking.

"You told me"—Herzoff spoke slowly—"that you had an offer to rent this house. Why don't you take it and get away for a month or two?"

Hannay bridled.

"Because a few silly women——"

Herzoff stopped him with a gesture.

"Your man Higgins isn't a woman, and he's not exactly silly. And I'm a scientist, Mr. Hannay, and I'm not stupid either. I have told you

before that, while I'm willing to accept evidence
or proof of spiritual phenomena, I am not by any
means superstitious."

Suddenly he raised his hand.

"Listen!" he whispered.

The tick-tick-tick of the death watch was distinct—a slow, rhythmical tapping. Herzoff went
to the wall and listened.

"It's here," he said.

He crossed the room and listened again at the
panelling there.

"It's here also," he said.

Then he turned and looked at the startled
householder.

"This is not a beetle, Mr. Hannay," he said
slowly, and looked at the watch on his wrist.
"It's just about now that one should hear it."

Hannay swallowed something.

"What do you mean?" he asked shakily.

Herzoff came back, pulled up a chair to the
round table that was in the centre of the room,
and sat down.

"Do you remember—or, if you don't remember, you've possibly heard—that there was a
murder committed on the adjoining property?"

Hannay nodded.

"Since you spoke to me I have been making

inquiries, and the general opinion seems to be that this wretched woman was not murdered where her body was found, but somewhere here, and to that murder I ascribe all these peculiar phenomena which you have witnessed or heard about."

Hannay felt a cold chill creeping down his spine. Yet it was hot, so much so that it was necessary to wipe his forehead of the moisture which had suddenly come there.

The Professor took a little package of papers from his pocket and opened them. They were typewritten.

"I'll give you all the facts of the case," he began. "I took some trouble to collect them . . ."

Upstairs in her room Pat had written her second letter. Her little desk was near the window, overlooking the garden. The desk itself was placed in a set of bookshelves that covered one side of the wall from the window to the door.

She had blotted the address when the rattle of stones against her window made her jump. For a moment she was too terrified to act, then, drawing aside the curtains, she pushed open the window. Beneath her she saw a figure, not difficult to recognize.

"How dare you do that!" she said unsteadily. "If you don't go away I'll call my father."

"I want to see you," said Peter earnestly. "It's terribly important."

She was less frightened now.

"Go away," she commanded angrily, "or I'll phone the police."

She did not see Peter smile.

"I'm afraid you'll find the wires are disconnected. You didn't know that, did you, but they're dead. I've a little instrument here"—he took something from his pocket that looked like a watch—"and I've taken the trouble to make a few tests."

It was all Greek to her.

"What do you want?"

"I want to talk to you. Will you come down?"

She shook her head.

"Then let me come up. I swear I won't hurt you or offend you in any way."

"Don't be ridiculous."

She thought for a moment, then:

"Go to the front door and knock, and I'll come down and see you in the dining room."

"No, thank you," said Peter, with the utmost politeness. "I never meet ladies in dining rooms; it spoils the romance. Let me come up."

Then she remembered.

"Who told you the wires were cut?"

"I didn't say 'cut,' I said 'disconnected.' Let me come up, only for a second."

Without waiting for her permission he jumped up onto the window sill below, caught a stout tendril of a vine that ran up by her window, and drew himself breast-high, his elbow on the sill. She stepped back and stared at him. She had a wild inclination to push him from his insecure foothold, for she supposed that his feet were resting on something.

"First of all, let me give you this."

He lugged from his pocket a book. From where he was he could just reach the bookshelf, and, by bracing his feet in a fork of the vine, could give himself the necessary purchase. He thrust the book into a vacant place on the shelf.

"Now listen, and don't interrupt," said Peter dictatorially. "I'm putting that book there because you may be in some danger. I want you to give me your word of honour that you won't touch it—until there is urgent need."

She was staggered by the request.

"Is this your idea of a joke——"

"It's no joke," said Peter. "The title's a joke

—it's called *Advice to a Young Lady of Fashion*—
God knows, you want no advice! You must
promise me you won't tell your father or anybody else that I gave it to you."

She looked at the dingy cover. Even at the
distance at which she stood she could decipher
the faded red title.

"What is it?"

She reached out her hand for it, but he stopped
her.

"Word of honour?" he demanded sternly, and
meekly she repeated the words.

Peter listened.

"Do you want to know why I'm hanging
round and why I forced my acquaintance on you
this morning? Oh, yes, I did it deliberately. I
could easily have avoided you. I was going to
slow the car, when I saw it was you."

"Why are you here?" asked Pat, and Peter
Dunn's face became suddenly stern.

"I'm here to clear the reputation of the best
man that ever lived," he said, and in another
second he had disappeared.

She looked down, but he was not in sight, and
she stood, puzzled and bewildered, until she
heard a sound that made her blood turn to ice.

5

The Professor was nearing the end of his narrative.

"They were tramps to the world, but they had known one another many years before, in happier circumstances."

He had a majestic delivery; gave to the most commonplace story the dignity of history.

"Both had deteriorated through the years, and he was a brute, more like a beast than a man. Then, one day, when they had touched the lowest depths, they met in this neighbourhood. The murder was committed"—his voice was slow and impressive—"in that wooden hut on the edge of your grounds. A witness heard the sobbing of the woman, saw the door of the hut open slowly, and the murderer come out."

He stopped for a moment.

"And that is what has been seen since."

Mr. Hannay shivered.

"I don't believe it——" he began.

"That is my theory," said the Professor. "She was in the hut when he found her. The sound you hear is not the tapping of an insect, it is the tapping on the door of the hut when the murderer sought admission."

His eyes suddenly travelled to the door of the library.

"Look!" he said huskily.

The door was ajar, opening slowly, without any human agency.

Hannay started to his feet; his legs gave way under him, but with an effort he braced himself and ran to the open door. There was nobody there.

"Who is it?" he asked hoarsely.

From the dark passage came the sound of a woman sobbing, and then a bestial scream that sent him reeling back.

Pat heard it and came flying down the stairs. She saw her father standing at the open door of the library, transfixed, his face pale, his mouth open ludicrously.

"What is it?" she asked.

"Did you hear anything?" demanded Hannay shakily. "This is the finish, Pat . . . we'll get out of this house to-morrow."

The Professor nodded slowly.

"That is the wisest decision you have ever made, Mr. Hannay," he said.

Morning brought a blue sky and a flood of sunlight, and Mr. Hannay weakened on his resolution. He came into Pat's little sitting room to talk the matter over with her.

"I don't know that I'm so keen to leave this place," he said. "In fact, darling, I feel I'm—um—running away from—not exactly danger, but the threat of danger. And we Hannays——"

For some reason Pat did not feel annoyed with him. She had some sense of protection which she could not define or explain.

Mr. Hannay, wandering about the room, his hands in his pockets, suddenly saw a new title on the bookshelf.

"What's this?"

He stretched out his hand. Pat hastily intervened.

"*Advice to a Young Lady of Fashion.* That's an old thing, isn't it? Who is the author?"

"I don't know who the author is," said Pat rapidly, "only I don't want you to touch it. It belongs to a friend of mine."

He looked at her suspiciously.

"It isn't one of those neurotic——"

"Don't be stupid, darling. It belongs to a friend of mine, and that is sufficient."

She asked herself, after he had left, why she had made such a scene, and exactly how important the wishes of the man called Peter were to her.

The Professor came down to breakfast with

them, but heard of Mr. Hannay's decision for the first time that afternoon. Pat found him walking about the grounds on her return from Maidenhead, where she had driven Mr. Hannay, who banked in that town.

"Are you admiring my car or our garage?" asked Pat.

Herzoff turned quickly and smiled.

"I didn't know you were back. Well, has your father let the house?"

She shook her head.

"No," she said quickly. "I have persuaded him to stay on."

He was taken aback by this.

"Do you know the story of this place?"

She nodded.

"Daddy told me on our way into Maidenhead."

"And you still wish to stay?"

"I still wish to stay," she said.

She felt a sudden antagonism towards this man—an antagonism which was unreasonable and unfounded. Herzoff chuckled.

"You're a very brave girl," he said. "I admire you for it, but I hope you will persuade your father to get out. You may laugh at me for a foolish, middle-aged man with illusions, but I am psychometric, and I have a feeling that this house at the moment is a place of doom for all of you."

"That's exactly the kind of house I like to live in," said Pat, with sudden recklessness.

On her way back to the house she passed the gardener. He straightened his back as she came near him, and to her indignation and amazement hailed her.

"Hullo, young lady! Having a chat with the Professor? He's a swell fellow! But he's not much better than me."

Then, to her horror, he put out his big paw and caught her under the chin, lifting up her head. She was paralyzed with fury. Then she struck at the big hand and went running towards the house.

Herzoff had been a witness of the scene. He came slowly across the garden. He was paring his nails with a small penknife, apparently intent upon his occupation, and he did not lift his eyes until he came face to face with the gardener.

"Don't do that," he said gently.

"Do what?" growled the big man.

"Don't touch that young lady."

Twice Herzoff's hand came up and down, and the gardener's cheeks went suddenly red and wet. The man uttered a roar and put up his hand to his slashed face.

"Don't do that."

There was a whimper in his face that was absurd in so big a man.

"There was no cause for that."

"Don't interfere with that young lady. Go and wash your face. Mr. Higgins will give you a little sticking plaster."

Pat came breathlessly into the kitchen. Mr. Higgins was putting glasses on a tray and looked round at her in surprise.

"Higgins," said Pat breathlessly, "who is this new gardener?"

"I don't know much about him, miss, but I'm told he's a very respectable chap——"

"Well, discharge him at once," she said.

"Why, miss, I'm sorry to hear you say that. He's not very presentable, but faces don't mean anything—that's my experience."

"It's dreadful that we've got to have men like that about the house," said Pat, as she made for the door of the dining room.

Higgins shook his head sadly.

"Well, miss, you can't get people to stay in a house that's supernatural. Personally, I don't mind, though it gets me worried at times."

Suddenly Pat remembered something.

"Where has he been sleeping—this gardener?"

Higgins hesitated.

"In the cellar, miss, but he won't sleep there now because of the noises."

"Have you the key?"

She put out her hand for it, and Higgins took it from his pocket.

"I wouldn't go down there if I were you, miss."

"I don't want to go down," she said sharply. "I want to lock the door so that nobody else can go down."

She tried the door; it was already fastened, and she slipped the key into her bag.

"That man doesn't sleep in this house to-night —understand that," she said.

"Very good, miss," said Higgins, a little hurt.

She saw Herzoff as she passed through the breakfast room.

"That man will not annoy you again, Miss Pat."

"I don't think he will," said Pat. "I've told Higgins to get rid of him."

His lips pursed.

"I assure you he's been punished enough——" he began.

"And I assure you, Professor Herzoff, that he will leave Chesterford to-day," said Pat.

There had been another witness of the incident in the garden. Peter Dunn had found a new point of vantage: a branch of a tree that overhung the little private road which was Mr. Hannay's very own. So situated, he could not get down to deal with the loutish gardener, but he had watched with some satisfaction and astonishment Professor Herzoff's summary administration of justice. He saw the girl and Herzoff go into the house, and waited. All that morning he had been hoping to meet her, and had his car conveniently parked so that he might follow and overtake her if she came out. And now, when his own machine was a quarter of a mile away, it looked as if he was to be baffled, for he saw her cross the lawn towards the garage, drawing on her gloves. There was no time for him to get his car.

Presently she came out, swept round the narrow drive near the garage into the road over which he was sitting. She was going slowly, which in a measure was an act of providence, for when he called her by name in a loud whisper she stopped the car and looked round, and, happily, stopped it right under the bough where he was sitting. She heard the thud as he struck the seat beside her, and looked round in amazement.

"Where did you come from——" she began.

"'Baby, dear,' you ought to say," said Peter. "And my answer is, 'Out of the everywhere into here.'"

"What are you doing here?" she demanded.

"Going for a ride," said Peter. "In America all the best gangsters take their friends for a ride."

"I'm not a gangster, and you're not my friend."

"Don't argue," said Peter Dunn. "Your father will come along in a minute, and he'll ask me my intentions. Think how embarrassing that will be."

She sent the car along with a jerk.

"You're a rotten bad driver, but you'll improve with practice."

"Why are those glasses round your neck?" she asked.

He wore a pair of field glasses suspended by a strap.

"The better to see you with, my dear." And when she shot an indignant glance at him: "A quotation from 'Red Riding Hood,'" he said gently. "Those glasses are for spying purposes. I've been spying on you."

She reached the secondary road and stopped the car.

"I've dropped my handkerchief. Will you get out?"

Peter shook his head with great calmness.

"That's a dirty trick to get me out."

"I don't want you here," she said.

Peter nodded.

"I know that. If you did, the whole thing would be simple. I should go to the registrar and get a license."

She gasped.

"Have you any sense of decency?" she demanded.

Peter nodded.

"Yes; that is why I should get a license first."

Again she stopped the car.

"Get out," she said firmly, and this time she meant it.

Peter obeyed. She did not drive on.

"I want to ask you one question. Will you tell me what is your name and why you are here? Probably there is some special reason why it should be kept secret, and if there is, I promise you I will tell nobody."

"My name is Peter Dunn," he said, after a moment's consideration. "Until yesterday I was

a sergeant in the Criminal Investigation Department of Scotland Yard."

He saw her mouth and eyes open.

"Aren't you any more?" she asked.

"No, I'm an inspector. I was promoted this
morning. They telephoned me—that is why my
manner errs on the side of frivolity."

There was a long silence.

"Why do you come here? What is there for a
Scotland Yard officer . . .?"

"A lot of things. But I'll tell you the main
thing that is keeping me hanging around here and
making me keep this case all to myself. I have a
personal interest in it—two personal interests:
one, the reputation of a dear friend of mine who
is dead."

"And the other?" she asked, when he stopped.

"The other is you," he said simply. "I'm
terribly sorry, but I've fallen in love with you."

His eyes looked at her straightly. He was
telling the truth. She went red and white, and
then:

"I'm sorry," she said.

"Are you telling the truth or a lie?" he demanded, the old smile in his eyes.

"I'm telling a lie," she said, and sent the car
forward in six distinct unworkmanlike jumps.

Peter was walking back the way he had come when he heard the hum of a car behind him, but did not turn round till she came abreast of him.

"I'll drive you back," she said.

"No, thank you," said Peter simply. "I'd rather walk."

She looked at him with disapproval.

"It's a very long way——" she began.

"You don't know where I'm going, so you can't say it's a long way or a short way."

"I don't like your manners."

"I've taken prizes for them," said Peter. "For the matter of that, I don't like your car. You've humiliated me."

She stared at him.

"Humiliated you? How?"

"I've told you I love you, and you haven't had the decency to fall out of the car into my arms."

She brought the car to a shuddering stop.

"Come here," she said. "You can kiss me— once."

He kissed her once, but it was a long once. . . .

Pat Hannay came back to the house. There was a look in her eyes that a wise woman could have interpreted. But there was nobody in Chesterford wiser than Joyce, the maid, and she at the moment was preoccupied.

Pat went up to her room, closed the door, took off her coat, and looked in the glass. There were some things which could not be believed. Some such thing had happened that day, and she could only look at herself in wonder. She found a difficulty in breathing normally, and the hands that tidied her hair were shaking.

She looked out of the window, hoping that by some miracle he would be in sight. . . .

There was his book. She reached out to take it, but remembered her promise and drew back.

A detective officer . . . a policeman . . . how would Mr. Hannay, somebody very important "in the drapery," accept that devastating fact?

Mr. Hannay had ideas for her; looked as high as the House of Lords; had confided to her his desire to found a lordly line with such assistance as she could offer.

A policeman . . . that puzzled her. She went down to the library to find some sort of reference book, having a vague idea that she could discover the briefest biography of the man who had kissed her once. For the time being, Chesterford and its horrible secret receded into the background.

The miracle did not happen: there was no

book more communicative than an annual
almanack which gave her the names and divi-
sions of some thirteen or fourteen superintend-
ents, but omitted any mention of Inspector
Peter Dunn, who yesterday was Sergeant.

Between then and dinner time she wrote him
a dozen letters, all very carefully considered, all
finishing on the first or the second page. One was
too dignified, another too friendly. She ran the
gamut of emotions, doubts, and hopes appropriate to the occasion. Happily she had secured
temporary help in the shape of a cook who had
come on the condition that she left the house
before nightfall. Chesterford was beginning to
gain unenviable notoriety, and Pat had almost
fallen on the stout lady's neck.

She had seen no more of the gardener, and
when she questioned Higgins, he told her that
the man had been paid off and had gone, and
she was a little relieved.

When her delirium had a little subsided, and
she came to take stock of her room—it was when
she began to dress—she became aware that
somebody had made a very careful search of the
apartment. The bureau drawer where she kept
her handkerchiefs was a muddle and a confusion
when she opened it. The drawers of her desk had

also been disturbed. Suddenly she remembered the key of the cellar, which she had put away in a pigeonhole behind a small table clock. The clock was there, but it had been moved. The pigeonhole was empty.

She finished dressing and went down to dinner but made no reference to the matter until they were in the drawing room and coffee had been served.

"Have you been to my room, Daddy?" she asked. "Somebody has been there, pulled out the drawers, opened my bureau, and searched my desk."

Herzoff looked up quickly from his coffee.

"Have you missed anything?" he asked.

"The key of the cellar," said Pat. "I took it from Higgins this afternoon."

Hannay had suddenly an idea.

"I wonder if it was that fellow—the man who is always wandering about this place—that young person. What did you call him——?"

"Peter?" said Pat incredulously. "Don't be stupid, Daddy. Why should he——"

Mr. Herzoff interrupted.

"Peter! What is his other name, do you know?"

"Peter Dunn," she said, and she saw the

Professor's mouth open and close and his lips draw in.

"Peter Dunn!" he repeated. "That's interesting. You know him, do you, Miss Hannay—a Scotland Yard man?"

"Hey?" Hannay was suddenly alert. "A Scotland Yard officer? What the dickens is he doing here?"

Pat rose to the moment heroically.

"He is my fiancé," she said, and the two men were dumb-stricken.

"Fiancé?" Mr. Hannay squeaked the word. "A policeman? Are you mad, Patricia?"

"I'm not mad," said Patricia. "I'm just telling you as a fact. He has asked me to marry him, and I'm going to."

She did not wait to see the effect of her pronouncement, but went up to her room. She had an uncanny feeling that Peter Dunn was near. Before she pulled the curtains and opened the window she extinguished the light. Her heart leapt as she distinguished a figure standing on the edge of the grass beneath her window.

"Is that you?" she whispered.

"That's me," said Peter Dunn. "*I* heard you!"

Her heart sank.

"Heard what?"

"I heard you telling your father that I'd asked you to marry me, which wasn't true. I haven't asked you to marry me. I merely made love to you."

"That amounts to the same thing in civilized communities," she said coldly.

She ought to have been furious with him, she told herself, but she did not feel furious. She had fallen instinctively into Peter's peculiar habit of thought and speech.

"I'm going to marry you, anyway," said Peter; "I decided that a long time ago."

She spoke to him again but had no answer. When she looked out he had gone. She thought she saw him in the shadow of a bush which grew against the house. Then she heard the crunch of heavy feet crossing the gravelled path. She could not see who it was, but he came nearer, and then her heart jumped. It was the gardener, the man Higgins said had gone, and he was coming directly towards her window.

She drew aside, peering round the edge of the window sash, and saw him halt on the lawn about half a dozen yards away. He was smoking a cigar; she saw the red glow of it as he took it out of his mouth.

"Are you up there, miss?" he asked in a croaking whisper.

She did not answer. Evidently he had heard her voice and had come across to investigate. What was he doing there? If Higgins had spoken the truth he had no right to be in the grounds of Chesterford. Perhaps he had come back for something he had left behind. She found a dozen uneasy explanations, and was relieved when he turned and walked back the way he had come, presently to be swallowed in the darkness.

"Your voice carries too far, young lady." It was Peter's sibilant whisper. "That was a narrow squeak."

"For me or you?"

"For me—therefore for you," said Peter. "Two guns, eh?"

"What do you mean?" she asked, bewildered.

"One on each hip—I saw them. Now go in, shut the window, and draw the blinds, and don't put on your light."

She sat in the darkness for a long time. Then she heard a sound that brought her heart to her mouth. A ladder was being put against her window. She sat and quaked. She had fastened the casement. She dared not look, and only a shadow, which almost seemed imaginary, showed on the curtain. Then she heard a soft, thudding sound, as though somebody was hitting a piece of iron with a hammer which had been carefully muffled.

Her first thought was to fly downstairs, but terror held her, and in her terror was that curiosity which is natural in a healthy girl.

After about ten minutes the hammering stopped. She heard the rasp of feet on the rungs of the ladder, and the scrape of it as it was taken away. She went carefully to the window, drew the curtain aside a fraction of an inch, and looked out. She could just see the man . . . it was the gardener!

Then she saw what he had been doing. Across her window stretched, in the shape of a St. Andrew's cross, two steel rods. They had this effect, that they made it impossible for the window to open.

Peter had seen the manœuvre, watching at a respectful distance. He waited till Standey had carried the ladder back to a big greenhouse, then he crept forward and saw the work he had been doing.

Something pretty bad was going to happen to-night. He wondered just what it would be.

He had a lot of work to do, and he had already

lost a considerable amount of time. He got back to the hut in the wood, fitted a jemmy together, and wrenched off the staple which held the door.

He was not unprepared for what he saw: a yawning hole in the middle of the hut, roughly supported by tree trunks that must have been cut for the purpose. A home-made ladder led to the depths. He went down quickly, reached the bottom, and saw the black mouth of a tunnel.

The floor was of rock and ascended; but the going was dangerous. At the very stir of his feet great lumps of earth fell from the roof, and he was glad to get back to the ladder and the outer air.

He reached the little lane and went on foot for a hundred yards. Near where he had parked his car four men were waiting for him.

"Well, Peter, have you found anything?"

It was the voice of his chief inspector, and with him were another Scotland Yard man and two heads of the Berkshire police.

"The whole gang is here," reported Peter. "Lee Smitt, Red Fanderson, and Joe Kelly. Smitt is posing as a professor with a knowledge of the occult. The curious thing is that he's been a member of this golf club for about twenty

years. He has probably visited the country before, and I shouldn't be surprised to find that
he's a member of some of the most exclusive
clubs in town. Fanderson's been working as a
gardener—I believe he did some gardening when
he was in Dartmoor—and Joe Kelly is back at
his old job—butler-valet, with the grand old
name of Higgins."

"We can pinch 'em," said his chief thoughtfully, "and charge 'em with returning to the
country after being deported——"

"I'm not here to pinch 'em for being deported," said Peter almost savagely. "I'm here
to wipe out the lie that put Sam Allerway into
a suicide's grave. That's highly dramatic, but
it's highly sincere. If you pinched them now you
wouldn't get the stuff. Eight hundred and thirty
thousand Canadian dollars, all lying snug."

"Where?" asked one of the Berkshire chiefs.

"In Hannay's house."

"I don't see how it can be in Hannay's house,"
said one of the men. "Why should they have put
it there?"

"I'll tell you why later."

"How did you stumble on this, Peter? When
you phoned me yesterday I thought you'd gone
crazy."

Peter Dunn told the story of the night when the little cruiser was tied up to Hannay's land.

"It was just a ghost story told by an hysterical maid," he said, "until the butler came down to return the rug. The moment I heard his voice I knew it was Kelly. I'd heard it in court—there was no mistaking it. I identified the gardener and Lee Smitt the next day. They've got nerve, but they're desperate. There are eight hundred and thirty thousand Canadian dollars, and that's a lot of money."

"Why should it be in Hannay's house?" The question was asked again.

"I'll tell you all about that one of these days," said Peter. "I'm going back now. Whatever is going to happen will happen to-night. I want the house closed on all sides, including the river."

"The Bucks police are sending a motor-boat patrol," said one of the Berkshire men. "I've got fifty plain-clothes officers within half a mile. When do you think you'll want us, and how are we to know?"

Peter Dunn explained his plan of operations; but, like many other carefully made plans, it was doomed to failure. Happily he did not know this as he went back quickly towards Chesterford and its strange guests.

6

When Pat went back to the drawing room she saw Herzoff shoot a quick, penetrating glance in her direction; then his eyes dropped. She realized he had seen that something had happened. She caught a glimpse of her face in a mirror: it was alight with excitement.

There was danger, here: she knew it. And Peter Dunn was at hand. That gave the danger a beautiful relish.

Her father was reading. Mr. Herzoff was working out a patience puzzle. Suddenly Hannay put down his book.

"I think I'll get another dog," he said. "I don't like the idea of your—" he made a wry face—"fiancé. That was a joke in the worst possible taste, Pat—wandering about Chesterford. It doesn't amuse me at all."

"What are you reading, Daddy?"

"One of the Famous Trials series. I must say it doesn't seem an appropriate book to be reading in the circumstances."

Herzoff looked up calmly.

"What is it called?"

He knew well enough what the title was; he had seen it.

"It's the trial of those three fellows who robbed the Canadian Bank of Commerce about ten years ago," said Mr. Hannay. "I suppose they got away with the money."

"I've forgotten what it was all about."

Herzoff went on dealing out the cards calmly and systematically.

"By Jove!" Mr. Hannay was struck with the brilliance of the thought. "There's a big haul for somebody. They got twelve years. I suppose they're out by now."

"They were deported," said Pat. "I read it in the newspapers."

Pat suddenly lifted her head.

"What was that?"

It was the sound of moaning, and it came from the window. Pat set her teeth, went across and pulled back the curtains with a jerk. She almost swooned. Framed in the window was the face of a woman, hideous, white, streaked with wet red. Her untidy grey hair was falling over her forehead.

With a scream the girl snatched the curtains back again and ran blindly back to her father. He had seen it, too.

"The tramp woman," said Herzoff in a low tone. "That is a manifestation I did not expect to see."

He spun round. From somewhere outside came the sound of struggle. There was a crash against the door that led onto the veranda, and then a single pistol-shot rang out.

It was Hannay who opened the door, and Peter Dunn staggered in. There was a streak of blood on his forehead; in his hand was an automatic. He closed the door quickly, turned the key, and for a second stood with his back to the door, eyeing two people who were amazed to see him and one who had murder in his heart.

Peter staggered across to the table and lifted the telephone.

"Dead, eh? Telephones don't have ghosts, Mr. Herzoff, do they?"

Herzoff did not reply.

Pat was by his side.

"You're hurt!" she said tremulously.

"Take my handkerchief—it's in my pocket," said Peter. "It's all right, it might have been worse."

"I'll get some water for you."

It was Herzoff who made this gesture.

"Yes, but don't trouble to get a priest; I'm not dead yet, Herzoff."

He watched the man leave the room, then he

lugged out of his pocket a clumsy-looking pistol, and handed it to Mr. Hannay.

"Do you mind taking this out onto your lawn and shooting it in the air? It's nothing more deadly than a Véry light, and I think you can go with safety."

He turned to the girl.

"Have you lost the key of your cellar?"

She nodded. She was not even surprised that he asked the question. By now Peter Dunn was the embodiment of all knowledge and understanding.

"I thought it might be the case. Will you get me some water?"

She ran into the dining room and came back with a glassful.

"Thank you, darling."

Mr. Hannay winced.

Peter drank the glassful at a gulp, and then, taking the girl's face in his hands, he kissed her. Mr. Hannay was petrified.

"What the devil do you mean by that?" he stormed.

"He meant to kiss me by that," said Pat quietly. "Didn't you?"

"Delightful," said a voice from the doorway.

It was Herzoff.

"You can lie down in my room if you wish, Mr. Dunn," he said.

He walked towards him leisurely, his hands in his pockets.

"I'm afraid you left an unpleasant stain on that door."

Peter turned his head. He did not feel the life preserver that hit him.

"Don't move, and don't scream, either of you!" snarled Herzoff. "And put that Véry light down, Hannay."

"What——" began Mr. Hannay.

"And don't ask questions. Come in, you boys."

The big gardener and the butler came in.

"Take him up to my room and tie him up. As for you, young lady, you can go to your room for the moment. When I want you I'll come for you. If you scream or try to attract attention, you'll wish you hadn't."

She walked past him, almost overtook the men as they turned into Herzoff's room, and presently reached her own. She slammed the door and locked it. She was dazed. Such things could not happen in England, she told herself again and again. She was having a bad dream and presently would wake up.

Mr. Hannay had submitted to being bound to a chair. To him the world's end had come. Here he was, in his own drawing room, being scientifically tied by a man whom he had regarded as . . . It was unbelievable.

"If I'd known who you were——" he said huskily.

Herzoff smiled.

"That's rather a foolish remark. After all, I've laid your ghosts: you owe me something for that. If you'd accepted the handsome offer I made to you when I wanted to rent the house, you would not have been troubled. Unfortunately, you very stupidly ignored that offer, and I had to frighten you—and you hadn't sufficient sense to be frightened."

He left his host and went up the stairs two at a time to his own room. Peter was lying on the bed, fastened hand and foot. He looked at him for a moment, then went on to Pat's room.

"Patricia!" he called softly. "It's Mr. Herzoff speaking."

She did not answer. He knew she had heard.

"I am the only person who can get you out of this house alive," he said. "Take a chance with me, and I'll keep the others off."

"I'd sooner die!"

He heard and smiled.

"Sooner have my gorilla, would you? Well, maybe you can have him. I don't know why Red has taken such a fancy to you, but women have been his weakness all his life. . . . I'm giving you a chance—do a little forgetting and come with me."

Again he waited for a reply, but none came.

"You don't suppose anybody's getting out of this house to tell the police who we are, do you? A great chance they've got! I'm phoning to a London newspaper to-night, telling them that you and your father have left for the Continent. Think that over—it means something . . . it means that you will not be found for a long time after I've left England."

When he got back to his own room he interrupted a flow of invective from the big gardener.

"That fellow took a shot at me!" growled Red Fanderson.

"If you'd been doing your job you wouldn't have been there," said Herzoff, and pulled up a chair to the side of the bed. "Well, Mr. Peter Dunn?"

"You'll go back for life for this," said Peter between his teeth.

Herzoff was amused.

"Why didn't you keep out of it? You've not been detailed; you took the job on as a holiday task, I understand. What do you want?"

"I want the money you stole from the Canadian Bank of Commerce, and a portion of which you made the judge believe Sam Allerway had taken. The money's in this house, under Hannay's cellar. You cached it here by accident. The other house belongs to you, doesn't it?"

He saw the man's expression change and chuckled.

"Got it first time! You bought the other house before you committed the robbery. I was checking up the dates. The night you got away from London in that second-hand car, you intended coming here to hide it in the cellar of the house you'd bought; but in the dark you went to the wrong house. They both looked alike in the days before Hannay started building—and one of you picked the wrong house, got into it, and buried your stuff under the cellar, and when you came out of quod you couldn't get it. You tried to build a tunnel from the gardener's hut, but the bedrock was too near the surface."

"We built the tunnel all right," growled Lee Smitt, and he was speaking the truth.

Peter was momentarily surprised.

He saw somebody standing in the doorway, watching him. He lifted his eyes and smiled at the hideous woman whose appearance at the window had so badly frightened Pat. Before she pulled off her tousled wig and began wiping the make-up from her face, he recognized the pretty Joyce.

"You might introduce me to your daughter, Smitt. She hasn't been through my hands—yet."

But Lee Smitt had other matters to consider.

"We've got to work hard to-night, Red," he said, "and get that stuff out. There's only another yard to dig."

"And hard you'll have to work!" mocked Peter.

Lee Smitt was looking at him with an odd expression. Presently he reached out and tapped the big "gardener" on the shoulder.

"Get that girl, Red. She's yours!"

Peter's face went white and drawn.

"If you hurt her . . ."

"If I hurt her or don't hurt her you'll be quite unconscious of the fact by to-morrow," said Lee Smitt curtly. "Help get him down to the cellar. There'll be a big hole there when those boxes come out, Mr. Dunn, and we'll want three people to put in it. That's all—three."

Pat heard their heavy feet as they carried Peter along the passage. And then she heard another sound—somebody was trying the handle of her door.

"Who is it?" she asked.

"Open the door, little darling."

It was the voice of the big gardener, and for a moment she swayed and had to hold onto the wall for support.

"You can't come in here. The door's locked. If you don't go away I'll scream."

"Sure you'll scream." The answer had seemed to amuse him. "You'll scream more in a minute. Open that door . . ."

The door shook as he threw his weight against it. She was terrified. She ran to the window, and then understood the significance of those two cross bars which prevented the window being opened.

A panel splintered under the fist of the big man, and she looked round in frantic despair. . . . Her eyes fell upon the book. *Advice to a Young Lady of Fashion.* It was a straw, and she clutched at it. She pulled the book out from the shelf. It was unusually heavy, and when she opened it she saw the reason: embedded in the very centre of the pages, which had been cut out to receive it, was a small automatic pistol. With trembling hand she took it out, and dropped the book on the floor as the door ripped open.

He was standing there, his face inflamed, his pale eyes like two balls of white fire.

"If you come near me I'll shoot!"

"Shoot, eh?"

He took one step into the room. The crash of the explosion deafened her. With horror she saw the man crumple up and go down with a crash to the floor, and she ran past him, still gripping the gun in her hand. The wonder was that in her excitement her convulsive clutch did not explode another shot.

She turned on the lights of the drawing room as she went in. Her father was sitting, trussed up in a chair. She tried to untie his bonds but could not. Then, on the floor, near the garden door, she saw the clumsy-looking pistol. She turned the key of the lock and ran outside. Aiming the pistol high in the air, she fired. It was an odd experience.

She was in the house again before the Véry light illuminated the countryside.

Where had they taken Peter? The library was empty. She passed into the kitchen and heard sounds. The cellar door was open, and she looked in. Then she heard the voices more clearly. It was Peter who was speaking.

"If you hurt that girl you'd better kill me."

"You'll be killed all right," said Herzoff. "Snap into it, Joe: we've got to be away from here by daylight. Joyce, you take the girl's car and clear—don't wait for us."

Pat walked onto the landing and took one step down.

"You'll ask me first, won't you?"

At the sound of her voice they looked up.

"Don't move or I'll shoot. Untie Mr. Dunn."

The quick-witted Joyce came sidling towards her.

"You wouldn't shoot a woman, would you, Miss Hannay?" she whined.

"If I had to shoot any woman I should shoot you," said Pat, and she so obviously meant it that the girl stepped back in a fright. "Untie Mr. Dunn."

She waited till Peter was on his feet, and her attention was so concentrated upon him that she did not see Herzoff's hand moving up the wall. If she had, she might not have realized that it was going towards the electric switch.

"Let's talk this over, Miss Hannay." The mysterious professor drawled his words. "Give us half an hour to get away, and nobody will be hurt. This stuff"—he pointed to an open door which evidently led to an inner cellar—"is ours. We've done twelve years for it, and we're entitled to have it."

And then the light went out. She heard a shot, and another, and the sound of a woman's shriek.

She flew up the stairs into the dark kitchen, and stumbled through into the open air. Somebody was at her heels. It was the butler. He grabbed at her and caught her by the sleeve. She tore her way out of his grasp and ran.

Somewhere near at hand police whistles were blowing. She had a dim consciousness of seeing men running across the lawn towards her.

"Where's Inspector Dunn?"

There was no mistaking the authoritative tone. She gasped her news.

Her pursuer had disappeared. They found him, when the lights came on, in the kitchen, a philosophical criminal awaiting the inevitable arrest.

As she came into the kitchen Peter staggered out of the cellar entrance.

"Have they got Smitt?" he asked.

She shook her head.

"I haven't seen him. You mean Professor Herzoff?"

Peter turned to an officer who had come in.

"Call an ambulance. He shot his daughter. If he didn't come up here he's down there still."

He looked at the butler.

"Is there another way out of here?"

"I'd say there is—through the tunnel, I guess," said Higgins sulkily.

"The tunnel?"

Peter remembered the man's boast.

"Yes, but it's pretty dangerous to use. The ground was too soft; it kept running down on us."

Peter turned quickly back to the cellar, reached the bottom of the stone steps, and passed through the door which separated the inner cellar. Then he saw for the first time the low entrance of the tunnel. Somebody was there.

"Come out, Smitt."

The answer was a shot that sent the earth scattering. It had another effect. Great lumps of soft earth began to pour through. Peter had just time to scramble back to the cellar when there was a rumble and a roar, and great clouds of dust shot out of the narrow entrance. He threw in the rays of his lamp, but could see nothing.

"That's the weakest part of the tunnel." It

was Higgins' quavering voice. "I told Lee we mustn't use it. . . ."

Suddenly he stopped, and a look of terror came to his face.

"Listen!" he whispered, and, listening, they heard the click-click-click of the death watch. "That's for Lee."

.   .   .   .

"There's nothing much more to explain," said Peter Dunn that night when he had told his story ostensibly to Mr. Hannay, actually to Mr. Hannay's daughter. "The first thing they did was to frighten away all the servants and substitute their own crowd. That was at the back of all the ghost business.

"They thought it would be easy. They had already made an abortive attempt to reach the cellar through a tunnel which they drove under the earth. It must have taken two months of hard work, and they used the time while you were in the South of France. They got into the house, but they didn't relish taking on the caretaker you left there, a policeman from the neighbourhood, if I remember rightly.

"Once they'd staffed the house with their own people, their job was to get rid of you and Pat.

They did the honourable thing—they offered to rent your house."

Mr. Hannay snorted.

"When that failed," Peter went on, "they used the method by which they had terrorized the servants to get you to give up your occupation. If you'd done that it would have been a simple matter: they could have opened up their treasure house at leisure. As it was, they could only work for a few hours a night, and they had to cart the earth away in sacks. You'll find two or three full sacks near your gardener's shed.

"What puzzled me was the maid, Joyce. I didn't know until this afternoon that Lee Smitt had a daughter who had been an actress. When she pretended that she'd seen a man walk through her room she acted pretty well. Anyway, she deceived you, Mr. Hannay, and I should imagine that you would take a whole lot of deceiving."

Pat tried to catch his eye but did not succeed.

"It is very remarkable how things come about," said Mr. Hannay. "Something told me that in no circumstances ought I to give up possession of this house—which shows you, Mr. Dunn, how the path of duty can also be—um—the path of glory. If I had taken the easier path we should not have captured these criminals. We might have saved ourselves a little trouble, and perhaps a little danger—and I don't think any of you realize how near I was to choking myself with that beastly gag the fellow put into my mouth—but we should not have had the satisfaction of having placed two miscreants in jail. By the way, I suppose my evidence will be necessary?"

"Undoubtedly," said Peter, with great gravity. "Your evidence will possibly be the most vital of all."

When her father had gone, Pat asked:

"Am I to go into that awful court?"

"You are not," said Peter Dunn emphatically. "There are quite enough people taking credit for this little coup. I will give all the evidence required, and if I'm asked I shall mention the fact that my wife was present."

"But I'm not your wife," said Pat.

"You will be by then," said Peter.

THE END